BIKE HUNT

A STORY OF T

Winner of the
**Young People's Books medal
in the Irish Book Awards**

'At last a teenage novel set convincingly in the urban setting. The plot is fast-moving, keeping the reader turning the pages right to the very end – and the characters are real and credible.'
CONSUMER CHOICE

'A fast-moving, action-packed thriller with all the right ingredients for the wide-ranging needs of this diverse age group.'
SUNDAY INDEPENDENT

An International success: translated into German, French, Dutch, Italian, Danish and Norwegian.

Fast-moving and exciting, BIKE HUNT will hold
your attention from beginning to end.

Hugh Galt is a journalist in Dublin.

He has also been a musician,

radio scriptwriter and fisherman.

This is his first children's book.

THE CHARACTERS

There's NIALL. Almost thirteen, very keen on racing bikes. The focus of much attention from the girls, but he's not aware of it yet.

And PAUDGE, his friend. Tubby, and a little less grown up than Niall. Sometimes a bit confused, he has his own problems to cope with, but he tags along with Niall, and contributes in his own muddled way to the hunt.

Then there's KATY. Superintelligent and an electronics expert. She leads the hunt. She is growing up too, and has her eye on Niall.

There are the TWINS. Coy and superficial, they too set their sights on Niall. But can their tricks match up to Katy's brains?

WASSERMAN, the German industrialist. He's kidnapped by an armed gang ... but not for long!

GASKIN and his armed accomplices. Tough and ruthless they are very angry at Wasserman's escape and desperate to find him.

PJ, and the bike thieves. They get caught up in the kidnap situation. . . .

BIKE HUNT

A STORY OF THIEVES AND KIDNAPPERS

HUGH GALT

THE O'BRIEN PRESS
DUBLIN

First published 1988 by The O'Brien Press Ltd.,
20 Victoria Road, Dublin 6, Ireland
Reprinted 1989, 1992, 1995
Copyright © Hugh Galt

4   5   6   7   8   9   1 0
9 5   9 6   9 7   9 8   9 9   0 0   0 1   0 2

British Library Cataloguing-in-publication Data
Galt, H.
Bike Hunt
I. Title
823'.914 [J]

ISBN 0-86278-157-4

Cover illustration: Massimiliano Longo, from the Italian translation
Book design: The O'Brien Press
Editing: Ide ní Laoghaire
Typesetting: Phototype-set Ltd., Dublin
Printing: Guernsey Press Co. Ltd., Guernsey, Channel Islands.

The publisher acknowledges the assistance of The Arts Council /
An Chomhairle Ealaíonn, in the publication of this book.

CONTENTS

CONTENTS

1

Stolen!

'IT'S GONE!'

It was one of those windless, overcast early summer days when everything seems to hang very still and quiet as if waiting for something to happen. And to Niall Quinn, it just had.

'My bike! Somebody's taken my new bike!'

The two boys stared in disbelief at the neatly snipped chain that had held Niall's gleaming new racer securely to the railings outside his friend Paudge's house only minutes before.

'How did they manage that?' Paudge wondered out loud. He resumed chewing whatever was in his mouth as his mind slowly began to puzzle out what had happened.

Niall looked each way along the street, but it was empty and deserted apart from a distant dog peeing up against a car. He bent down, pulled the chain from the iron railings, and examined the broken link.

'They must've used a bolt cutter. Damn!!'

He threw the chain on the pavement with an angry clatter. Paudge took a small step or two out of the way, just in case. Although both boys were exactly the same age, almost thirteen, Niall was much bigger and more strongly built than Paudge, who was more the short and round type. In fact in earlier times, before Niall's frame had begun to fill out, friends used to tell them they looked like the figure 10 walking down the road together. And Paudge knew from childhood-long experience that although Niall hardly ever lost his cool, he would more than likely go raging mad when he did.

'What'll we do now?' asked Paudge. He could see the jaw muscle twitching angrily just below Niall's ear.

'The guards', said Niall. 'We'll get the police after them!'

He led the way back into Paudge's house and went straight to the phone. Paudge's mother stuck her head round the kitchen door at the other end of the hall when she heard the tense footsteps.

'Anything the matter, dear?' she asked apprehensively. Although she looked the fat and jolly type, she was in fact an acutely nervous woman who picked up any tension around her like a radar scanner.

'Niall's new bike's been knocked off. They used a bolt cutter,' Paudge explained with a certain amount of irritation. Things were bad enough, and he didn't want his mother fluttering anxiously around making them worse. But she came straight out of the kitchen, wiping her flour-covered hands on her apron, her forehead in a nervous knot.

'Oh, that's terrible! That beautiful new bike he only got yesterday? That's dreadful, shocking! How did it happen? What's his father going to say? We'll have to do something!'

Niall was already explaining the facts to the policeman at the other end of the phone.

'It's a 19½ inch racing frame, 12 speed, all Shimano 105 alloy equipment, narrow sprint racing wheels, pearl white with metallic blue and yellow markings .... The number? No, I haven't ... it might be at home on the guarantee card. I'm at a friend's house ... But it was only stolen a few minutes ago, if you get after them right away you'll catch them! ... Yeah .... OK ..... OK.'

He banged the phone down and turned to Paudge. 'He says they can't do anything without the frame number. We'll have to go over to my place and get it straight away. Is your old BMX still out in the shed?'

Paudge nodded and led the way to the back of the house, taking something from his pocket and stuffing it in his mouth on the way. Paudge's mother watched them anxiously. 'Be careful!' she advised them pointlessly as they went out by the kitchen door.

There were two BMX bikes in Paudge's shed, a fairly new one and a smaller one that had seen a good deal of use. Niall took the older machine even though he was the bigger, and pedalled aggressively out the side gate of the house onto the road. Paudge followed as close as he could, chewing faster. As they turned right in the direction of Niall's house, which was about a mile away, a girl ran out of a gate on the other side of the road, waving frantically at them.

'Niall! Stop! I've got something to tell you!' she shouted.

She was lanky, almost as tall as Niall, and had dull orange hair pulled back tightly into a long pony tail. In her excitement, her glasses were slipping off her lightly freckled nose. She ran into the middle of the road and watched as Niall accelerated away, head down, without acknowledging her call. She held something small aloft in her right hand, as if she wanted to show it to him.

Paudge looked back, swerving violently as he did so.

'Can't stop, Katy!' he shouted back at her. 'Niall's just had his new bike robbed!'

The two riders sped out of sight round the corner, leaving Katy standing with her arm still up in the air, a roll of film in her hand.

'I know that!' she shouted after them, stamping her foot in annoyance. 'Eejits!'

★　　　★　　　★

Niall's dad was washing the dishes when the two lads trudged in gloomily from their visit to the garda station.

'Hiya, boys!' he greeted them cheerily as the plates rattled in and out of the sink. 'How'd it go then? She's a real flier, eh?'

Niall sat heavily in a chair at the kitchen table, trying to avoid his father's eyes.

'Somebody stole it', he said quietly. Paudge could see Niall was close to tears, and he felt suddenly anxious and embarrassed.

'Stole it?' Niall's father echoed with slow disbelief. 'Oh no.'

Niall stuck his hands in his pockets and stared intently at his crossed feet through water-filled eyes while his father stood looking at him, soapy bubbles dripping off the ends of his fingers. There was silence for several seconds and Paudge felt as though he was going to explode. Without thinking he snatched a biscuit from a plate on the table and began munching it noisily, then shrank into his chair when he realised what he had done.

'What happened?' asked Mr. Quinn, drying his hands on the apron he was wearing.

'I chained it to the railings outside Paudge's house for a few minutes. When we came out, it was gone. The chain was cut', Niall explained, still staring at his feet.

'Did you see anybody?' asked Mr Quinn. Both boys shook their heads. 'Did you tell the guards?' Niall nodded.

'We came back here and got the frame number just before you came home,' Paudge explained. 'But they said that even with that, there's not much they can do except hope that it turns up. Hundreds of bikes get stolen every month.'

Mr Quinn sat down between them at the table and let out a long breath. 'Well of all the . . .' he said quietly. 'And you only had it one day. Did you even get a chance to try it out properly?'

Niall shook his head. 'I'd just gone round to see if Paudge wanted to come out with me. When we came out . . .'

Mr Quinn shook his head, and put his hand on Niall's arm.

'I know there's not much I can say that'll help at this stage, Niall,' he said. Paudge sneaked another biscuit. 'But we'll do our damndest to get it back. And if it turns out in the end that we can't, we'll buy another one. Okay?'

'It took us a year to save up for this one, Dad,' said Niall.

'I know,' Mr Quinn agreed ruefully.

'And I traded in my BMX against it. Now I've got no bike at all and the summer holidays start in two weeks.'

Mr Quinn pursed his lips and made a helpless face. Paudge knew it was going to be a problem for them to get the money together again. Niall's father used to be a sports journalist on one of the big papers, but then he got some disease with a strange name that paralysed him every so often, so he had to leave his job and stay at home. Niall's elder brother Joe had just started university, so the whole family depended on Mrs Quinn for their income. She was something in a computer firm, and worked very hard, hardly ever seemed to be at home at all in fact. Paudge wished his mother would get a job like that.

The doorbell rang.

'I'll get it,' said Mr Quinn, glad of the interruption. Paudge used the opportunity to guzzle the last three biscuits on the plate.

'Got any Seven Up or something round here? I'm thirsty.'

Niall pointed to a cupboard, and Paudge was on his way to it when Mr Quinn opened the kitchen door to let Katy in. Niall looked up.

'Hi, Katy,' he greeted her without much enthusiasm.

'Katherine,' she corrected him patiently.

'I'm afraid Niall's not feeling very friendly at the moment,' Mr Quinn told her. 'His brand new racing bike's just been stolen.'

'I know,' she replied coolly. 'I saw it happen.'

Paudge nearly let the Seven Up fall on the floor. Niall sat bolt upright in his chair.

'You did?' said Mr Quinn. 'Would you recognise the thief again? What did he look like?'

'Like this,' said Katy, as she took something carefully from her pocket and laid it on the table. It was a colour photograph of a man bending down beside Niall's bike and doing something with the chain. Mr Quinn and the boys bent over it, astonished.

'Careful,' Katy warned them. 'I printed it only a few minutes ago. The surface is still soft.'

'That's amazing!' said Mr Quinn. 'How did you get this?'

'I was upstairs at home trying out a new telephoto lens Daddy got for our camera when I saw Niall come along and lock up his new bike, and then this man appeared, cut the chain and rode off on it,' Katy explained. 'I took a couple of shots of him, then ran downstairs to call the garda station, but I dialled for ages and still couldn't get through. When I ran out to tell Niall what I'd seen, they just zoomed off.'

'How did you get the picture printed so fast?' asked Mr Quinn.

'I developed and printed it myself in Daddy's darkroom. I learned how to do it from watching him and from reading his books. It's not that difficult, really,' she said.

Paudge gaped at her and took a deep swig from the open bottle. The bubbles went up his nose and made him snort.

'There's a better shot drying at home,' she went on. 'You can see the man's face from the front in it. Will we get it and take it to the guards?'

Niall was already up and on his way to the door.

'Hang on,' said Mr Quinn. 'We'll all go together.'

11

'They're great pictures all right,' said the officer at the desk. 'You did a great job, Miss.'

'Will they make your job any easier?' asked Mr Quinn.

'That's the big question,' the officer smiled wryly. 'I'll have to pass these on to the detectives to see if any of them recognises this character. If he's one of the known gangs, then there's a chance all right.'

'Gangs?' echoed Paudge.

'Gangs is right,' said the officer seriously. 'Bicycle thieving's got very organised these last few years, almost an industry you might say. There are a few gangs going round the city nowadays, mostly in vans. They hit one area one day, another area the next and so on. It's no problem for them to steal ten or even twenty bikes in a morning.'

'Do you know who they are?' asked Niall.

'Well, most of them are known to the police all right. The big problem is to catch them at it, and even that's not much good. If you nab one stealing a bike, all you can do is charge him and let him go, and he's at it again the next morning. The only cure is to smash the organisation behind the thieves, and that takes time.'

'So even with the pictures ...' began Niall.

'Well, you never know,' said the officer, leaning forward on his elbows to study the photos. 'But I don't want to raise your hopes. Even if this man is caught tonight, God knows where the bike'll be.'

Niall seemed to shrink at least two inches as his shoulders slumped. Mr Quinn put an arm around him.

'I'll just take your name and address, Miss,' the garda said to Katy, 'and somebody'll come round and get a statement from you in a few days. Meanwhile, we'll hang on to these photos of yours.'

★　　　★　　　★

'You know what?' Paudge told Niall through a mouthful of crisps, 'this would probably never have happened if you'd done what I said and bought yourself a new BMX instead of a racer. Nobody steals BMXs. Least I never heard of gangs going around in vans to steal BMXs.' He stuffed his face with another fistful of crisps.

'That's because the BMX craze is over,' said Katy. 'Nobody really wants them any more.'

'Who says it's over?' retorted Paudge, deeply offended.

'I read about it in the paper,' Katy informed him. 'Apparently sales of BMX bikes collapsed to almost nothing last year.'

'Crap! I don't believe it!' Little bits of half-chewed crisp were spraying out of his mouth and down the front of his sweatshirt. 'BMX is still the greatest! Isn't it, Niall?'

Niall sat morosely on the steps outside the kitchen door, throwing bits of gravel into an empty plant pot beside the path.

'Who cares?' he said through barely moving teeth.

Two girls on bicycles appeared at the gate to the lane at the end of the rear garden. They looked identical, with neat blond hair and gleaming white clothes.

'Hey, Niall!' one of them called. 'We're going up to the castle. Come on out and show us your new bike!'

Paudge cringed internally, and tried to signal to them to shut up, but his contortions only made the newcomers start giggling.

'What's up, Paudge?' called the second girl. 'You got constipation again?' This made them laugh out loud.

'Go away, you two!' Katy ordered. 'Niall's not feeling well. He doesn't want to be bothered with clowns like you!'

The twins stopped giggling instantly. 'And you can go back to your encyclopaedias, you specky-faced swat!' jeered the first one.

Niall stood up suddenly and threw a handful of gravel into the vegetable patch. 'Why don't you all get lost!' he snapped irritably, and slammed the kitchen door behind him.

'Now see what you've done,' Paudge scowled at Katy.

$$\star \qquad \star \qquad \star$$

Niall went up to his bedroom and shut the door behind him. The walls of the small square room were covered with posters, some of them showing BMX riders in their spacemanlike protective gear performing flying manoeuvres, others, newer, showing the stars of road-racing — Hinault, Kelly, Lemond, Fignon, Roche — in the painful throes of battling towards a variety of finishing lines.

He went over to the window and leaned his head against his arm on the glass. Outside, through the gaps in the houses, he could see the afternoon city bustling away in the distance below. Somewhere down there somebody had his new bike, and there was nothing he could do about it.

He turned away and leapt onto his bed, and began punching the pillow madly with both fists.

2

Tuning In

'WOW!'

Paudge surveyed the attic room and its contents with flabby-lipped astonishment. Niall stood behind him, silent but no less impressed, as Katy held the door open for them and watched their reactions with carefully controlled delight.

'Now remember, Paudge,' she intoned sternly, 'keep your sticky fingers in your pockets and don't touch anything. If my dad notices I've had anybody up here, he'll go spare.'

'They're not sticky,' Paudge protested mildly, but he put them in his pockets anyway and entered quickly before she could think of any other reason for barring him. The room was surprisingly large, with narrow windows on two sides set into the sloping walls that were the underside of the roof. All round the sides were benches, shelves and cabinets packed with electronic equipment, control panels, component boards, stripped-down TV sets, trails of cable, boxes of bits and pieces, and dozens of other bewildering items that the boys couldn't even begin to fathom. One corner housed what was evidently a radio station with a number of transmitters and receivers stacked neatly in high racks behind a small table on which stood a microphone and a morse key. On the wall nearby was a thin plastic box about two feet square, the top surface being a very peculiar map of the world, circular, with the British Isles at the centre. In the middle of the room, taking up virtually all the floor space was a workbench where at least a dozen unknown items were undergoing repair or construction, and it was littered with components, tools, baffling little boxes that looked like transistor radios covered in bright knobs, and sheets of incomprehensible diagrams.

'It's like the inside of a space station!' said Niall as he and Paudge wandered fascinatedly in different directions. 'What's it all for?'

Katy closed the door and kept her eye on Paudge while she explained. 'Oh, a lot of it is just junk — things that Dad brings home from work so he can cannibalise them for spare parts.'

'He's a computer programmer or something isn't he?' said Niall.

'Not at all,' she told him, a bit surprised that he of all people could be so ignorant on such matters. 'He's a maintenance engineer — that's the hardest job of the lot, probably even harder than design and construction. You need to be really topnotch to be able to figure out what's wrong with a computer in the first place, then track down the fault and put it right. Not everybody can do it.'

Niall was only half listening. He had found what looked like a big electric typewriter with a roll of paper attached to the top.

'What's this?' he wondered.

'It's a teletype terminal,' Katy explained. 'The old fashioned kind they used to use in newspaper offices before everything went digital. It still works — watch.'

She went over to the radio station and turned a few knobs, then went to the teletype machine and pressed a couple of switches. A few moments later the terminal started to clatter and lines of words unfolded on the paper.

'It's from Singapore!' Paudge said excitedly as he squeezed between the other two for a closer look. 'What's it about?'

'Oh, it's probably some financial stuff. It's tuned into one of the press agency frequencies, and that's what they go on about most of the time.' She switched it off again, and Paudge looked as though he was about to protest, but didn't. 'Dad's a radio ham, and he used to be dead keen on collecting stuff like this and getting it to work again, but now he doesn't really have the time. He just goes on the VHF bands sometimes at the weekends to talk to his pals. Says it's cheaper than using the phone.' She pointed in the direction of the radio station.

'Hey, look!' interrupted Paudge, leaning over the teletype terminal to get a better view out the window behind it. 'You can see into my bedroom from here.' He pointed across the tops of the small trees lining the road outside to his house on the other side. It was a neat two-storey Victorian terraced house with big windows, identical to Katy's except that it had no attic room, and the paintwork was a different colour.

'I know,' said Katy, trying hard to control a smile. 'Especially when you have the light on and you forget to close the curtains.'

Paudge turned a pale shade of scarlet and his toes curled up inside his grubby runners. When they were changing for gymnastics at school, he'd recently noticed that Niall was beginning to sprout some curious hairs below his belly, and every night before he got into bed, Paudge had a good look — sometimes with a magnifying glass — to see if the same thing was happening to him in the same place. Maybe Katy had ...

'And do you understand all about this stuff?' Niall had picked up one of the big sheets with the incomprehensible drawings from the workbench and was bending his head from side to side as he tried to spot something even remotely recognisable in it.

'My dad's teaching me,' said Katy enthusiastically, and she turned the diagram the right way round for him. 'I know it looks difficult, but once you've got a few of the basic formulas it's all surprisingly simple really. I'm studying for the radio amateur's exam, and my dad says I'll have no bother getting through it in a couple of years. Then I can get my own callsign and operate the station myself.'

Niall was looking at her with such concentrated wonder that she felt suddenly intensely self-conscious and pushed her black-rimmed glasses hard up to the top of her nose as she always did in

16

such circumstances. Paudge, at the other end of the room, turned round to see what all the silence was about. The sight of Niall's dark brown eyes gazing deeply into the lenses of Katy's specs made something clench inside him, and he felt an overwhelming compulsion to put an end to whatever was going on.

'Paudge! Stop that!' Katy sprinted over to where he was experimentally flicking switches on the various bits of the radio station. 'I warned you not to touch anything — you'll destroy it all!'

She pushed him violently aside and put the switches one by one back to their off positions. But Paudge's attention, and Niall's, were locked in amazement on the thin plastic map box on the wall. A narrow beam of light had appeared from the centre of the circular map to its edge, and was moving slowly round the coloured countries like the second hand of a big clock.

'What's that?' they both asked at the same moment that Katy hit the switch to turn it off.

'It's a beam direction indicator,' she told Niall, but not Paudge. 'It shows you which continents the rotating antenna stack outside is pointing towards.'

They gaped out a window into the long back garden, at the end of which was a narrow tower about the same height as the house. It was made from what looked like thin scaffold tubes welded in crosses and squares, and at the top was an array of rods and cables like several outsize TV aerials one on top of the other.

'Wow,' Paudge commented quietly.

'How does it turn?' asked Niall, intrigued.

'There's a geared electric motor on top of the mast,' Katy told him, keeping a hostile eye on Paudge. 'Watch.' She pushed down a switch next to the radio station and the light beam on the wall map came on again and started moving. At the same time, the aerial array on top of the mast in the garden began to swing round at the same slow speed.

'That's fantastic!' admitted Niall. 'And does it only send signals in the direction it's pointing in?'

'You get a little bit of power off the back of the stack, but most of it goes straight out the front — nothing at the sides at all. It's the same when you're receiving.'

'But how does it work?' Niall wondered, his mind wide open. Katy drew in a breath to begin her explanation, but changed her mind when she saw Paudge pull something from under one of the circuit diagrams on the workbench.

'Hey! This is a walkie-talkie!' he announced, delighted to have found something he could put a name to.

'It's a hand-held transceiver and put it down!' she snapped, and whipped it from his grasp before he had the chance to obey. But Niall had found another one on a nearby shelf, and was inspecting it with equal pleasure.

'Do they work?'

'Not at the moment.' She took it away from him too, but respectfully. 'My dad's modifying them so they'll have a bit more power.'

'How's he going to do that?'

'Bigger power transistors in the final amplifier, and an external battery pack to give them more juice.' She kept a sideways eye on Paudge, who was hovering dangerously close to the morse key. Niall considered what she said with blinking eyes and parted lips, and nodded dumbly. 'They'll have a much longer range when he's done that,' she went on. 'Ten miles under the right conditions. Maybe more.'

'Maybe we can test them out together when they're ready,' Niall suggested keenly. She seemed to think this was a good idea, and seemed to be about to say so, when Paudge's hand finally reached out for the morse key. She got to it before he did and gave him a staggering shove towards the door, indicating that the visit was over.

'You'll have to get out — my mum'll be back from the hairdressers any minute!'

Paudge seemed happy enough to have to leave, but he protested anyway. 'She's only just gone!'

'I know,' said Katy, steering him towards the door with a series of short pushes, 'but she's got very short hair. Now will you please get out quick!'

Niall followed after them reluctantly, looking round as he went at various items he hadn't had a chance to investigate. 'Maybe we can come back again some time,' he said hopefully.

'Maybe,' agreed Katy, who had successfully steered Paudge to the top of the narrow stairs and appeared to be fighting the temptation to give him the final push.

'Come on, Niall,' urged Paudge, with a jovial smirk. 'Let's go up the castle and have a bit of fun. The weather's too good to be hanging about indoors.' He galloped down the steps to the bedroom landing, and then on down to the front door where he rewarded himself by unwrapping a few sticks of chewing gum from the store of provisions in his pocket.

'What are you going to do at the castle?' Katy asked Niall on the way down. The place in question was an old, ruined tower on top of a nearby wooded hill where the youngsters of the area traditionally went to play out their childhood fantasies. She herself hadn't been near the place for about two years, and she was a bit surprised at the idea that Niall still frequented it.

He grinned as though he could read her thoughts. 'Ah, we don't play hide and seek or tag any more like the old days. We just . . . mess about. You know . . .'

'Mess about at what?' she insisted.

'Well . . . we've got a couple of ramshackle ramps for the BMX stuff. Sometimes we play football. Sometimes we light a fire in the old tower and roast some sausages for fun. Otherwise we just . . . mess about.' He shrugged and smiled at her, but after her response to the smile had faded, she still had the feeling that there was something she hadn't found out yet.

'Maybe I'll come with you,' she announced without looking back at him. Paudge, following the conversation at the bottom of the stairs, quickly shoved the chewing gum to one side of his mouth.

'What d'you want to come with us for?' he demanded. 'We won't be doing anything that'll interest you.'

'Paudge's right,' agreed Niall. 'We'll only be messing, and I don't think that's your scene, really. You'd probably be happier upstairs studying your electronics books.'

'But the three of us always used to go playing up at the castle together,' she objected, somewhat offended at the implications of his words.

19

'That was years ago,' Niall reminded her.

'Yeah!' agreed Paudge, chewing again now that Niall was on his side. 'We were only kids then. Things have changed. Some of us grew up.'

Katy looked at him askance. 'Well,' she said after some pursed-lip thinking. 'Maybe I'll just go up there myself. You can't stop me.'

Paudge shrugged nonchalantly. 'We'll just go somewhere else, won't we Niall?'

'Okay, I'll do a deal with you then.' She addressed herself to Niall. 'If you let me come up with you, I'll give you a loan of the walkie-talkies when they're fixed.'

'Done!' said Niall immediately. For a few moments, Paudge tried to think out the possible consequences of such an agreement, his jaws moving slowly. But the mental effort was beyond him so he gave up and nodded wary approval.

3

The Castle

THE CASTLE was deserted and silent when the three rode up and dismounted in front of it. Even in its heyday in the twelfth century, it hadn't been a real castle, just one of the plain, square towers dotted all over the Irish countryside by invading Norman knights to allow them to keep a feudal eye on the lands they had stolen from the unwelcoming natives. Now it was four crumbling walls about fifteen feet high, with a low doorway at the front, and higher up a few narrow slits for windows. It stood almost on the crest of a hill and still commanded a fine view of the slopes, once pastoral but now thickly housed, that ran down to the south edge of Dublin Bay, where the grey sea lay like a docile dog in the protection of the heavy-shouldered mountain of Howth to the north. Behind the castle, on the hilltop, was a ragged unkempt bit of a wood whose ancestor could well have been planted by the first Norman lord of the manor to give his stone-cold home some protection from the biting Irish breezes. A few stragglers from the mass of trees, scrubby oaks and alders and other semi-civilised growths, formed a rough pair of arms around the remains of the tower, almost enclosing a bare slope about sixty feet across in front of the little door. This would have been where the courtyard was, where the steel-clad nobleman with the foreign tongue was helped onto his charger by squires and vassals before thundering off downhill to slice up some scruffy Danes or decapitate a few Irish chieftains with unpronounceable names. At least, that was how the scores of youngsters who came to play here on the sunny summer days imagined it.

But the hoofmarks of noble steeds were only an ancient memory now. Instead, the bare earth was criss-crossed and circled by the crazy tracks of knobbly bicycle tyres, for this was where the local BMX freaks came to skid, race and practise their often dangerous stunts. At the bottom of the slope was a ramp made from heavy timber that could once have been a shed door. The high end of this ramp was about four feet off the ground, and about six feet further away was a slightly lower heap of hard-packed soil which sloped downwards.

'See?' said Niall. 'There's nothing much going on here.'

'So, what are you going to do then?' Katy insisted.

Niall pulled down the corners of his mouth and shrugged, and then suddenly shot his bike — Paudge's old BMX machine — diagonally down the slope towards the wooden ramp at breakneck speed. Katy clenched her stomach muscles involuntarily as he sailed off the end of the ramp, standing on the pedals, then came down perfectly on the earth slope. He sprinted back up the slope and skidded the bike back into the precise spot from which he'd started. Paudge smiled approvingly.

'That's about it,' Niall informed her laconically. 'We just belt up and down like that for hours on end, trying to figure out something crazier to do than the last time. Not very intelligent, really.'

Paudge started to trundle down towards the ramp, but slowly, standing carefully over the handlebars for full control of the machine. About ten feet from the ramp, he suddenly sprang forward onto the front part of the frame and pirouetted the entire bike round so that he and it were travelling backwards. In this position, he continued on to the ramp, rolled about halfway up it till the bike's slow momentum petered out, and then balanced stationary for a brief moment with his hands high above the bars before gravity started rolling him forward again. He finished the performance with the same uphill sprint and skid-stop that Niall had demonstrated.

Katy was astonished and impressed, and her face showed it plainly. Paudge, ever since she first met him in the junior school all those years ago, was somebody she had always thought of as clumsy and awkward and ungraceful. Now here he was performing acrobatic feats with the smoothness and agility of an East German gymnast on the telly. It was a shock.

'How did you learn that?' she demanded of him.

Paudge bunched up his face in an exaggerated smirking smile. 'Not from sitting at home reading books anyway.'

From behind them came a stifled sound that could have been a chortle. They all looked round but there was nothing there other than the tower and trees.

'Must've been a bird,' suggested Niall, and then he was off downhill again, out of the saddle and head down. This time, after his soaring leap across the ramps, he halted the bike on the way back up, and without putting his feet on the ground, laid it over on one side while he balanced on the frame. Then, moving his feet deftly, he swung the bike vertically upwards so that it was balancing on its broad back tyre while he stood on the back tube of the frame and bounced himself and bike up and down with one hand in the air. Paudge applauded.

'That's called a cherrypicker,' he informed the gaping Katy. 'Niall's the only freestyle rider round here who can do that every time.'

From behind them came another muffled sound, this time vaguely like a cheer.

22

'I think there's somebody in the tower,' Katy told Niall as he skid-stopped beside her again.

'Let's go see,' he suggested. They laid their bikes down on the least churned-up area, and Niall led the way up to the black doorway. He leaned his head inside, holding onto the lintel with one hand. 'Who's there?' he demanded with mock seriousness. 'Come outa that and show yourselves!'

There was a distinct laugh this time, or rather two laughs in unison. And mingled with that distinctive sour odour that the insides of ruined buildings always give off, Katy's nose could detect the faint but pungent smell of something burning.

'Come in and get us!' came back the challenge from the dim interior, and it was a voice that Katy recognised. Niall and Paudge ducked in straight away, and Katy followed cautiously, picking her way across the rubble and junk underfoot. Inside, flanking what in days of yore must have been the huge stone fireplace at which the noble lord warmed the seat of his chain-mail pants, were two crude benches made from bits of planks and small oil drums. And seated grinning on one of them were the twins.

'Hiya, Niall! Hello, Podgy!' They looked at Katy with a snigger. 'What's that ya got with ya — a giant bookworm on legs?'

'Ah give over!' Niall ordered as he and Paudge moved forward to the benches in a manner that suggested they were familiar with the situation and the procedure. He hauled one of the twins from her perch on the plank and pushed her towards the other makeshift bench and Paudge then sat down by the other sister and began bum-hopping sideways till she was squashed, giggling in protest, between him and the crumbling wall.

A surge of anger and strange embarrassment coursed through Katy as she watched the smile on Niall's lips and the unfamiliar look on his face. So this was why he was so vague about the meaning of messing about. It had never occurred to her to ask him who he was messing about with. The very idea just never entered her mind ...

'Come on in and have a seat,' Niall invited her. They were all looking at her and she became aware that her cheeks were burning. She felt another surge of anger, this time at herself for feeling angry, and then another for being unable to hide her anger. She wanted to get out of this place as fast as she could, but instead she sat down meekly on the end of the bench occupied by Paudge and Judith. Or was it Gwynneth? They were so identical and always so identically dressed she could never tell which was which. Nobody could, and she knew they derived deliberate glee from confusing people. She felt yet another stab of rage over that.

'What's the crack, then?' Paudge inquired jovially as he offered round a packet of fruit gums from his pocket.

'The biggest crack around here is in your head!' spluttered the twin next to him, and she and her sister went into sniggering convulsions while Niall and Paudge looked on bemused and Katy glowered at their shameless display of juvenile emptyheadedness.

'It's you two that's cracked,' said Niall, luxuriously excavating his left nostril with his middle finger. 'What've you been up to recently?'

'Upstairs and downstairs and in my lady's chamber,' lilted the one beside him, and again they both writhed with hilarity at this obscure piece of wit. Niall and Paudge exchanged brief grins, and then grabbed the twins roughly and began twisting their arms and necks.

'Come on! You've been at it again! Tell us!' demanded Niall. The twins squirmed and squealed in protest, the one in Paudge's grip putting more effort into it than her sister, who pulled out a five pound note from somewhere among her clothing and waved it around as a kind of surrender flag. Niall snatched it away and let her go.

'Where did you get this?'

'She took it out of a drawer in Ma's bedroom!' blurted her sister before she had a chance to say anything herself. Niall looked at her.

'Is that right, Gwynneth?'

'Judith,' she corrected him as she shook her ruffled blond hair straight again, smirking defiantly. 'Yeah, I did! The old bat won't miss it — she's got rolls of money lying about all over the place.'

'That's stealing!' Katy felt the words fall out of her mouth before she could do anything about it, and immediately clamped her jaw shut. She knew the twins had a totally spoiled attitude to money and material things. Their parents had loads of money — the father was a businessman and the mother had her own boutique in town — and they lived in a huge house with enormous landscaped grounds on the other side of the hill. The twins always had everything they wanted, and if they heard anyone else express a wish for something, they usually went and got that too just so they could be envied even more. She was quite sure they didn't have to steal any money, they could have as much as they wanted just by asking. They probably took it just for the devilment.

The twins looked at her with a momentary amused sneer, then turned away disdainfully. Gwynneth, the one next to Paudge, produced a black packet, and with theatrical exaggeration, opened it, pulled out a long white cigarette and pushed it into her pouting lips.

'You're not going to smoke that?' protested Paudge. She didn't reply, but produced an expensive-looking cigarette lighter and proceeded to light up, head back and eyelids fluttering, while her sister sniggered.

'I suppose you ripped them off too,' said Niall.

'We don't need to rip things off,' rejoined Judith as Gwynneth awkwardly blew out her first mouthful of smoke. 'They're lying around the house and we take them. Nobody notices they're gone.'

'Like a puff, Podgy?' Gwynneth inquired mischievously, holding the cigarette out to him. He looked at it misgivingly, then at Niall who was watching impassively, then took it and stuck his head forward to put it in his lips.

'Don't suck too hard, Podgy — you might swallow it!' Judith giggled. Paudge took two small puffs, smacked his tongue at the taste, then hurriedly gave the cigarette back as he spat disgustedly into the rubble at his feet.

'Come on, Niall, you try!'

Niall put his hands under his thighs and shook his head vigorously. 'No way!' he said firmly.

'How about Madam Einstein then?' said Judith. The twins turned to Katy.

'Yeah!' said Gwynneth. 'Take a good deep puff, my dear!' She

25

got up and held the cigarette in front of Katy's face, forcing Katy to lean back.

'I don't want it. Take it away!'

'Shy, are we?' said Judith, joining her sister in front of Katy. 'Give her a bit of help then, Gwynneth!'

Gwynneth took a deep suck at the cigarette, obviously not enjoying it as much as she had been pretending to, and blew a cloud of smoke straight in Katy's face. Spluttering with distaste, Katy jumped up and made for the low door, but before she got there, a wave of raucous yells penetrated from outside. Niall and Paudge stood up together.

'Who's that?' wondered Niall. He skipped past Katy to duck out first, and the others followed, the cigarette tossed forgotten in a dark corner.

Outside, they all stoood blinking as their eyes readjusted from gloom to full daylight. On the slope in front of them, a gang of about half a dozen boys were racing around on bikes, some BMX, some battered street machines. The BMX riders were leaping the ramps while the others simultaneously shot through the gap between the two ramps, heads and shoulders hunched down.

'It's Pedro,' observed Paudge with ominous flatness in his voice. Niall stood still, his narrowed eyes following the obvious leader of the intruders, a boy of the same age and build as himself, wearing a BMX helmet and gloves, and shouting orders and curses at the others as they pedalled madly round in their respective circles. The twins crowded close to Niall, their eyes full of excitement.

'Are you going to fight him, Niall?'

'Yeah! Tell him to get off our patch — they don't belong here!'

Niall paid no attention, but kept on watching with his arms hanging by his side. Suddenly Paudge erupted.

'My bike! That guy Brophy's got my bike!' He bolted off towards one of the riders who was sprinting back up from the ramp, and dragged him to a halt. 'Get off!' he yelled. 'That's my bike!'

The girls and Niall watched tensely as Paudge struggled to wrest his machine from the offender, who didn't take too kindly to being manhandled.

'Quit shovin' me!' warned the boy with a snarl.

'Get off my bike!' Paudge insisted, and pulled the frame so that the boy toppled backwards and landed with a painful-sounding thud on his back. Paudge pulled the bike protectively close to him, but the boy jumped up and swung an angry punch at the middle of his chest, sending Paudge and the bike staggering back. Crimson with rage, Paudge swung the bike aside, and on the way back threw an almighty right hand straight into the face of the oncoming unfortunate who fell over again, clutching his head with both hands.

Katy watched all this with increasing anxiety, fearful of what she seemed certain to have to witness next. All the other riders had stopped to watch this exchange, and seeing their man getting the worst of it, had dropped their bikes and were closing in vengefully on Paudge, who looked pleadingly at Niall.

Jaw tight and twitching, Niall set off down the slope with long, hard strides. Seeing this, the pack encircling Paudge halted, waiting to see what he was about to do. Niall bulldozed through the middle of them, getting only black looks in return for the rough shoves he gave to any who stood in his path. He continued to the wooden ramp, where Pedro, like a general, was standing back to let his troops take care of the problem. Without words or hesitation, Niall let fly several ferocious fists at the frozen Pedro's stomach and face, sending him flying sideways with his legs tangled in his bike.

'What was that for?!' he demanded from the ground, blood appearing at the corner of already swelling lips.

Niall looked down at him for a second, then turned and marched back up to Paudge. The other boys moved back this time, and he picked up Paudge's bike. 'Is it okay?'

Paudge nodded, and they both went back to where the girls were waiting at Niall's and Katy's bikes. Their eyes were sharp and their faces white.

'Let's split,' said Niall, and he led them, walking, along the path down the hill, not even bothering to look back. When they were well out of sight behind the bushes, the twins and Paudge let out long phews of relief.

'I was getting worried there,' admitted Paudge.

27

'Yeah!' agreed Judith. 'There were so many of them!'

Niall looked over his shoulder, but nobody was following them. Then he looked at his fist, which had two or three raw spots on the knuckles. Then he gave them all an impish smile. 'Always go for the jugular,' he advised. 'Come on, let's get moving before they get themselves together and change their minds!'

'We've no bikes!' protested the twins.

'Hop up on the pegs,' Paudge suggested. Both girls tried to climb onto the pegs projecting from the rear axle of Niall's bike, but Gwynneth got there first, so Judith hopped on behind Paudge. Both stood upright and held onto the shoulders of the riders.

'Let's go an' get some burgers with this fiver!' said Gwynneth.

'Great!' said Paudge. 'I'm ravenous!'

'Coming, Katy?' Niall asked her.

'No,' she said after a short pause.

'There's no homework in the summer holidays!' jeered Judith, but Katy only looked at her coldly.

'See ya around then!' Niall called to her, and sped off down the track with Paudge close behind and the twins giggling again.

Katy freewheeled carefully down to the road, and then pedalled thoughtfully in the direction of home. She was just beginning to realise she actually did have a lot of homework to do.

4

Stop Thief!

TWO SATURDAYS LATER, Niall spotted the bicycle thief.

He and Paudge had gone into town on the train with the intention of spectating at a cycle race in Phoenix Park. True to her word, Katy had lent them the beefed-up walkie-talkies once her father had finished working on them, and the two boys planned to position themselves at different points along the course and keep each other informed by radio as to how things were progressing at their respective ends. Paudge was excited over the walkie-talkies — they'd tried them out in Niall's garden the night before and they worked fantastically — but the weather had gone windy and wet overnight, and since the race was an adult road bike affair and not BMX, his enthusiasm for it was not as steadfast as Niall's.

'It's going to rain again,' he forecast authoritatively as he looked out at the scudding clouds above a station where the train halted and at the puddles on the platform. 'We'll get soaked.'

Niall didn't reply. He was watching a group of girls who were waiting for the carriage doors to open to let them in. They were a bit older, probably fourteen, all dressed in new gear for the Saturday's trip into town, and buzzing with high spirits. They piled in and charged towards a group of seats further down the carriage, squealing and giggling exuberantly. Niall, sprawled low in his seat and with one hand over his mouth, swivelled his eyes furtively between the girls and the window.

The train moved off, producing more screeches from the girls as one who was still standing toppled onto the others. Paudge turned his head round in the direction of Niall's narrow-eyed gaze, and gave them a disdainful twitch of the nose.

'Eejits!' he muttered. 'You'd think they'd have grown up a bit by that age.' He turned back to Niall. 'What d'ya think, then?'

Niall's eyes switched back and forth between Paudge and the gigglers. 'Eh?' he finally queried.

'About the weather. The rain.'

'Rain? Oh . . . ah, we'll see what it's like when we get there.'

Another explosion of raucous mirth from behind Paudge made him turn his head again, this time to see two of the girls trying to pull something from each other's hands and falling out of their seats in the process. He turned away disdainfully, only to find Niall again watching them with furtive fascination, so he snatched up a newspaper somebody had left on the seat beside him and flung it open with noisy irritation. At first he threw the pages over and scanned them with no real interest, but then something caught his attention, and soon he was deep in concentration.

The train sped on, the girls chortled and cavorted, Niall spied on

29

them, and Paudge read. Two or three stations further on, the doors of the carriage shot open to admit a horde of pensioners taking advantage of the free travel period. Small portly women with tightly curled white hair and luridly powdered faces swarmed in and claimed their seats, defiantly clutching their handbags on overfed knees while their feet dangled an inch or two off the floor. With them were a few shrunken husbands, carefully parcelled in overcoats, scarves and caps on even though it was early summer, their faces either blank with tedium or full of nervous wonder at what was happening to them. Two women crashlanded on the seats beside Paudge and Niall, and Paudge jumped as he felt the walkie-talkie clipped to his trouser belt being squashed into his flank. He gave the woman a scathing look, which she ignored, and pulled the radio round till it was next to the battery booster pack on his other side. The women began complaining indignantly to each other about the disgraceful weather as Paudge leaned forward to Niall with the paper in his hands.

'There's an amazing article in here about what sportsmen should eat,' he informed him. Niall was only half listening. In the now crowded carriage, the girls were harder to observe, and besides, it looked as though they were getting ready to disembark. Unheeding, Paudge proceeded to expound. 'It says most of the top athletes have gone off meat, and they usually go for vegetables, rice and pasta. What's pasta?'

'Spaghetti. Macaroni. Things like that.' Niall's head was shifting about as he tried to see between the bodies blocking his view. Paudge digested the definition of pasta for a brief moment, then continued.

'But you should see the list of things they say you should give up: butter, milk and cheese — too much of them gum you up, it says. White bread, cakes, biscuits — anything with white sugar in it. Anything processed, in packets or tins. And listen to this.' He looked up for emphasis. 'Chocolates and sweets are banned entirely.'

'Why?' asked Niall. The train was stopping and the girls were messing around at the door. Paudge consulted the page again.

'Well, apart from the sugar and the milk products, there's all

30

sorts of chemicals used to make them — colouring and stuff — that ruins your liver and things. It says they're like low-level poisons.'

Paudge seemed genuinely aghast. The train had stopped and the girls spilled out. Niall took one last look through the window as the train pulled away again, and then pulled a face of disbelief. 'They can't be that bad. Gizza look.'

He took the newspaper and opened it as far as the bulk of the gabbling woman next to him would allow. Paudge stared at the big, meaningless headlines on the front page as he ruminated on the import of what he had just read. He felt in the pockets of his jacket, where four heavy Mars bars lurked guiltily among the other tongue-tempting toxics he'd bought in a rush at the station shop just before they'd left. Poisonous? He felt mild horror at the thought of how much must have gone down his throat in his lifetime. Maybe it was already too late ...

'Tcha!' Niall crumpled the paper dismissively, drawing behave-yourself stares from the two old women. 'If it was all that bad, we'd be dead by now,' he pronounced.

The women stiffened at the mention of the word, and Paudge took back the newspaper, carefully removing the relevant page and folding it neatly to fit in his inside pocket.

'Can't be wrong if it's in the paper,' he protested softly.

Niall got up, knocking into the women's legs with blithe unrepentance. 'Come on — this is our stop.' Paudge followed obediently, but as he did so the train braked to a halt and plonked him right in the lap of one of the old dears, causing her to emit an oooomph of pained indignation. He disentangled himself and bolted before she had time to recover and launch a verbal counter-attack.

Niall was waiting at the station exit, holding his collar tight around his neck and looking up at the weather with a face of screwed-up resignation. 'You might be right, you know,' he admitted. 'It's getting worse all the time.'

Paudge made no reply. He headed straight for a litter bin and began throwing the now forbidden contents of his bulging pockets into it in a mercilessly determined manner, eyes bright with the power of self-discipline. He had finished before the dumbfounded

31

Niall could overcome his amazement and stride across to stop him.

'Have you gone off your head?' Niall pushed him aside and stuck his arm deep into the bin to retrieve the discarded provisions. 'What d'you want to do a thing like that for?'

Paudge was very composed. 'I'm giving them up. They're a health hazard. The paper said so an' I believe it.'

'Listen,' Niall told him as he stuffed his own pockets with the goodies, 'my da worked on a newspaper all his life an' he says half what's in them is bullshit!'

Paudge shrugged. 'Well that just means half of it isn't bullshit, an' I think what I read belonged to that half.'

'What's all this sudden concern about health anyway?'

Paudge readjusted the walkie-talkie ensemble on his belt, and pulled the buckle in a notch. 'I just want to stay fit, that's all.'

'Fit? For what?' Niall tore the wrapper off a Mars bar and aggressively took half of it off with one bite. Paudge turned and looked out into the rain.

'You never know. Maybe one day I'll want to try pro cycling myself. You can't be a pro cyclist with a poisoned liver.'

Niall's jaws, engaged in close combat with the Mars bar, gave out a grunt of ridicule that sounded more like a cow pulling its foot out of the mud. He chewed hard for a few moments, then swallowed. 'Come on, we'd better figure out what we're going to do now.'

They both stared at the downpour now thrashing the road outside.

'Looks like it's in for the day,' pronounced Paudge. 'Maybe we'd better just go to the pictures instead.' He pulled the folded newspaper page from his pocket and poured over the advertisements on the reverse side from the article. 'There's a Star Wars kind of a thing on at two o'clock in the Carlton.'

Niall looked at the rain again and let out a long snort of disgust. 'Okay. Let's go, then!'

'Hang on a minute.' Paudge turned round and went towards the station kiosk. 'I just want to get some apples.'

When he came back with a bulging brown paper bag in the crook of his arm, Niall was standing out in the downpour to get a better look at another gang of boisterous girls going past.

'If you go on like this,' Paudge commented drily, 'next thing you'll be taking a fancy to old Professor Four-Eyes.'

Niall intentionally misaimed a kick at him, then turned and sprinted off along the road. 'Come on!' he shouted back. 'Or we'll miss the start of the film an' I'll have to work it all out for you again!'

Paudge took an apple from the bag and threw it at him before thundering off in pursuit.

★   ★   ★

Old Professor Katy Katherine Four-Eyes was at that moment still in bed, even though it was lunchtime, and even though she was a habitual early riser who got up at 7.30 a.m. prompt every day, even Sundays. She lay on her side, watching and listening to the rain spattering on the window. Dad was out on a job, and Mum had gone shopping in town with a friend, so Katy had abandoned her usual route and got back under her eiderdown to Think About Things.

Things had been knocking her ordered existence apart recently and she had been concerned about them for quite some time. Some kind of slow upheaval had been taking place in her life which she wasn't in control of, and this annoyed her. She'd begun to notice it a few months before, when Dad first allowed her to use the attic workshop while he wasn't there. She was supposed to be studying electronics and monitoring morse transmissions so she could pass her radio amateur's exam, but keen and dedicated as she was, something kept unsettling her, and she found her attention continually wandering to the window whenever she heard voices out in the street. Boys' voices. And one voice in particular: Niall Quinn's.

She had tried determinedly to discipline herself at first, but the compulsion grew stronger by the day until she was forced to the inevitable conclusion: she was in love. Or rather she was the victim of an adolescent infatuation. She'd read about these things in various books she'd come across — purely by chance — in the library, so she knew the difference and the respective symptoms.

The only thing the books had never divulged, however, was what to do about it.

She had decided, in that case, to work it all out for herself the way you do in mathematics, from first principles. If you're thirsty, she reasoned, you don't ignore the thirst and hope it'll go away. You go and get yourself a drink to cure the thirst. So if you're in love ...

Next step had been to draw up a plan of campaign, a step by step list of logical steps leading to the solution of the problem, the way Dad did it when he was working on a wonky computer. So she had taken a pencil and a piece of paper and sat down and wrote:

Objective: Niall Quinn.

She sucked her lips and thought for a moment, then wrote:

Obstacles: 1. The twins. 2. Podgy.

Then after another lip-sucking pause for thought and a glance in the mirror:

3. Me.

Next she wrote, in block capitals: ACTION: and sat and waited for her brain to tell her what to do. That was the way she solved mathematical problems — just stared and stared at the question till the solution popped out of her mental silence. But this time ... zero, nil, nothing. Very annoying.

And then one night came the weird dream. She had dreamt she was on a sea-fishing trip with her dad on the rocky coast of west Clare where they often went on holiday. They were fishing off a rock ledge into a deep swell when Katy hooked an enormous silver fish that thrashed and twisted in the foam. The fish was so strong she felt afraid she was going to be pulled in, so she shouted to her dad to help her. But it wasn't her dad who came, it was Niall. He put his arms round her and they both pulled and pulled and pulled against the battling fish until ... the line snapped and they both fell over in a tangle. At first they were dazed, but then they started laughing and Niall leaned forward to kiss her ...

It was after this disconcerting fantasy that Katy had decided it was time to seek expert advice, so she had paid a call on Cousin Fiona. Under the duvet, Katy wriggled into a different position and grinned to herself as her memory began rerunning the mental video of that eventful meeting.

Cousin Fiona was fifteen, not quite two years older than Katy, but Katy felt sometimes it might as well be two hundred. That was because Cousin Fiona was so knowledgeable about Things. Not about chemistry and physics and electronics and photography and maths, the way Katy was, but about the real mysteries of life — clothes, fashion, hair styles, make-up, pop culture, parties, and of course, boys.

Cousin Fiona had a new boyfriend virtually every week, sometimes two at the same time, once even three. Katy had always regarded her amorous antics with distinctly disdainful fascination, being totally baffled as to what any sensible female would do with just one boring boyfriend let alone three. And it wasn't as if Cousin Fiona was any raving beauty. She was a short, muscular, broad-shouldered redhead whose legs, Katy had often thought, looked like the ones you see on the heavy dining tables in old people's houses. True, she had a dazzling smile, stunning blue eyes, and her blouses bulged. But in her altered state of consciousness, Katy was now deeply suspicious that there was more to it than just that, so she had presented herself meekly before this expert captivator of males, ready and willing to erase all former prejudices from her memory and be appropriately reprogrammed for the task she had set herself.

'Hiya, Kate! Jeepers, are you still wearing those awful frumpy clothes!' Fiona was always refreshingly blunt to friend and foe alike, but rather than making her unpopular, the habit seemed to have just the opposite effect. Katy keyed this item into her memory for subsequent evaluation.

'Hello, Fiona,' she began. 'I . . .' She waved an arm helplessly at her outfit, unable to offer any convincing explanation of its quite obvious drab and tasteless qualities in contrast with Fiona's fresh, bright and brashly fashionable ensemble.

'I know, I know.' Fiona smiled consolingly and put a friendly and powerful arm around her blushing cousin. 'C'mon upstairs an' we'll have a chat about it. How's the crack anyway? We haven't seen you for months — what brings you round these parts, eh?'

Katy tried to think of some way of saying why she'd come without actually saying why she'd come, but she didn't have to bother. Fiona's life revolved round the very things Katy wanted to hear about and the conversation immediately turned in that direction with no need for prompting on her part.

'Ruth's upstairs with me,' chirped Fiona. Ruth was her current best friend. In fact she had dozens of best friends, and favoured different ones on different days, depending on her mood, the weather, and what she was up to, rather like queens used to do way back in history. Fortunately she was so universally popular none of them really minded.

'We're going out on a double date with a couple of new fellahs tonight,' she explained as she guided Katy into her bedroom. It was an unbelievable mess. Katy had often been in it before, of course, but the sheer magnitude, the totality of the disorder took her breath away every time. The floor was ankle-deep in books, clothes, magazines, bags, shoes, records, empty and half-empty coffee cups, the odd plate or two with the mummified remains of a sandwich or a piece of cake, and other bits and pieces that had long since ceased to be anything you could put a name to. The bed was a crumpled heap, the chairs were full of cast-off garments, and the bookshelves and all the other surfaces were overflowing with chaos. Right up on top of the curtain pelmet, a forlorn pair of pink knickers were gathering dust. The walls of the room — Fiona had painted them herself, garish yellow, all streaks and brushmarks — were almost covered by posters of pop stars and groups, some of them dressed and made up like circus performers, the others mostly deliberately scruffy-looking characters with grim scowls that were no doubt meant to be very macho, but made them look to Katy as though they had just had their bums smacked.

In the midst of all this, at the dressing table by the window, with a cassette player bopping away on one side and a vase of collapsed flowers on the other, sat Ruth, calmly and carefully applying thick make-up to her eyes. She was quite the opposite of Fiona — tall, very slender, generally admired for her cool elegance. Looking at her and Fiona, Katy was reminded of tall lean Niall and squat wobbly Paudge, and wondered why so many people choose their opposites for friends. She keyed this item into her memory too, for later evaluation.

'Hi there, Katy!' Ruth turned to smile the greeting at her and exposed her one serious flaw, a mouthful of small brittle-looking teeth rather like a baby's milk teeth. It's true, nobody's perfect, Katy thought to herself with a certain amount of satisfaction as she glanced quickly at herself in the mirror while she returned the hello.

'What're you into these days?' Ruth inquired with an impish little smile. 'Astronomy, is it? Or philosophy?'

'Electronics,' Katy informed her uncomfortably, hiding her eyes behind the frame of her glasses. 'Just for a pastime.'

Ruth grinned. 'Ah well, enjoy it while you can. It won't be too long now before all your time will be taken up with this kind of thing, eh?' She turned back to her image in the mirror and went on with her engrossing task, neck stretched out and eyes blinking.

'Don't mind her!' chuckled Fiona as she swept some debris off a chair to let Katy sit down. Katy had once asked Fiona if her mother didn't object to all this mess. Her? Fiona had replied incredulously, have you ever seen her kitchen? Katy had had to admit it was a valid comment.

'Ruth's only jealous because there's nothing inside her head 'cept fellahs an' fashion,' Fiona went on cheerily. 'There's lotsa chicks around that would give an arm an' a leg to have your brains, pet. They could do somethin' decent with their time instead of trundling around at the heels of some idiot boyfriend, eh?'

Ruth let out a chortle of ridicule and Fiona, curled up on the bed, aimed an elderly running shoe right at the middle of her back. Katy got an uncomfortable tense feeling in her insides at the mention of the word boyfriend, and Fiona homed in on the vibes straight away.

'You haven't got a boyfriend, have you, Katy?' Fiona asked suspiciously. Ruth turned round in anticipation. Katy shook her head with the vigour of truth, but her eyes squirmed under the mental X-rays in the gaze of the other two girls.

'Is there somebody you fancy then?' demanded Ruth.

Katy sat rigid and blushed. Fiona's and Ruth's mouths dropped slowly open, then they looked at each other before intoning together: 'Kaaaaaaty!!!'

They both leaped in unison across the mess and hauled the helpless Katy onto the bed, where they bounced her and themselves up and down and over and back, squealing and shrieking with amazement and delight.

'I don't believe it!' gasped Fiona after several minutes of this. 'I just don't believe it!! My brainy little cousin's just like the rest of us after all!' She threw her arms round Katy and they fell off the bed together in a tight hug.

'What's he like?' Ruth demanded to know. 'Go on — tell us! Blond? Blue eyes? She and Fiona giggled almost to choking point.

'He's ... he's called Niall,' Katy blurted out as she struggled from the floor. Fiona and Ruth exchanged a suddenly serious look.

'Oh well, I don't suppose it's his own choice,' Fiona shrugged philosophically, and dragged both herself and Katy back onto the bed. 'So that's why you're here, eh? You want us to tell you what to do about it?'

Katy smoothed her skirt and adjusted her glasses. 'Don't get the wrong impression — I'm not that bothered at all, actually ...'

Fiona gripped her tightly by the arm and looked her intently in the eye. 'Here's my first piece of advice, Katy: don't fight it. It'll only get you in the end, and struggling'll leave you too exhausted to keep the upper hand. Understand?'

Katy nodded her assent to this piece of logic.

'And my advice is to do something drastic about yourself,' said Ruth, before she bounded over the bed and started tugging off Katy's school blazer. Katy was about to fight her off, but Fiona laid a reassuring hand on her shoulder.

'Relax, Katy, we're only going to give you a little live demonstration on how to revamp your image a bit — get a little pzazz into you. Clothes, make-up, hair, that sort of stuff.' Ruth had started undoing Katy's pony tail while Fiona explained. 'And while we're doing that, we'll give you a crash course on how to handle yer man: how to get him, what to do with him when you've got him, and how to dump him when you've had enough of him. Okay?'

Katy had smiled a little smile of shy pleasure and nodded meekly ...

She was still smiling when she became aware again that she was still lying in her bed, that it was lunchtime, and that her empty tummy was roaring for food. Outside, the rain had stopped, and suddenly the sunlight was blasting in through the window, so she leapt out from under the duvet and threw the window wide open. A great wave of wet summery smells washed over her — warm damp soil, pungent plants, that delicious odour of a summer shower evaporating off the hot tarmac of the roads. She closed her eyes and stood basking in the rays of the sun, smiling a wide smile of sheer physical delight. Life was getting better all the time ...

★   ★   ★

Down town, the sun was shining too, but Niall wasn't feeling quite so good about it.

'Damn!' he muttered as he and Paudge emerged from the dark enclosed otherworld of the cinema into the eyewrinkling sunlight. 'We should have gone up to the park after all. They ran the full programme, I bet you they did.'

Paudge paid no attention to his peevishness. The film they'd just seen was still playing in full glorious technicolour in his head, and he was mad keen to head straight for the nearest place where they could act out the scenes of intergalactic mayhem that impressed him most.

'We'll go up Stephen's Green,' he announced and set off without waiting for a reaction. 'We'll use old Katy's walkie-talkies. Full power on the main propulsion!' And off he sprinted, making imitation jet noises. Niall followed unenthusiastically, but knowing full well that when Paudge got all revved up like this, the only thing to do was to tag along till he burned himself out.

The aimless herds of Saturday shoppers in Grafton Street slowed him down a bit and gave Niall the chance to look in a few windows at hi-fi gear and android-looking female dummies in skimpy swimwear. Paudge sneaked a few glances at his reflection in the shopfronts to see if his new no-junk regime was having any effect on his waistline yet, and thought he could see the beginnings of an improvement already.

39

'I need a burger,' Niall announced gruffly as they walked through a cloud of frying aromas outside a Macdonald's joint.

'Suit yourself,' Paudge shrugged haughtily, and devoured his last apple while Niall went in to get himself a quarter pounder and large fries.

With this inside him, and a can of Coke to wash it down, Niall was in something of a better humour when they reached Stephen's Green. The sun was burning fiercely in a cloudless sky now, and although the paths were dry, the morning's downpour was evaporating strongly from among the thick flowerbeds and the copses of bushes and trees in the neat little park, making the air feel and smell distinctly jungle-like. Little children were showering the ducks in the duckpond with sackfuls of bread, while fathers took off their jackets and rolled up their sleeves and mothers spreadeagled themselves on the benches, bare legs unhealthily white in the strong light, twisted toes poking through the straps of their sandals.

'You go up to Harcourt Street corner and I'll go over near the swings,' Paudge suggested. He pulled his walkie-talkie unit round to the front, ready for action.

'Okay,' Niall agreed. 'Gimme a couple of minutes, then call me.'

He jogged off through the strolling crowd, and Paudge trotted in the other direction. Paudge could swear he felt already lighter on his feet after his morning of self-denial, but although there were a full two pounds of apples in his belly, he could sense a dangerous hunger gnawing its way up through him. Then the sharp memory of the taste of crisps suddenly filled his mouth, and he found himself veering south towards the shops as if in the grip of some invisible extraterrestrial power. He forced himself to turn back, but although his legs were taking him in one direction, his stomach seemed to have taken on a life of its own and was exerting a strong force in the other.

'Stop that, will you!' he snapped angrily at his navel, causing a family walking past to stare at him. He veered off the path into a clump of trees, and slumped back against a sloping trunk.

'It's him, Paudge! It's him!' came an excited, squawky voice from under the front of his jacket. A wave of cold terror washed over him for a brief second as he imagined his innards were now actually talking back to him, but then he realised it was Niall calling him on the radio.

'Blast him with your laser!' Paudge answered, once he had fumbled the apparatus off his belt and into action. He assumed that Niall had started straight away into an interstellar drama.

'No, you eejit!' Niall snapped back. 'It's him! The bicycle thief!'

'The who?' Paudge was completely disorientated.

'The guy who stole my bike! He's walking down the outside of the Green looking at all the bikes chained to the railings!'

'How d'you know it's him?'

'I've got that picture Katy took of him. I always carry it with me. Just in case.'

Paudge stared nowhere for a blank second, then shouted: 'Get the guards! I'll get the guards!'

'Cool down, will you!' the walkie-talkie ordered. 'Listen. He's coming in your direction. I'll trail him and you nip out and look for a guard. There might be one walking up and down outside the Shelbourne Hotel. Hurry!'

'Roger!' Paudge acknowledged, and sprinted for the nearest gate out of the Green. He zoomed down to the corner opposite the Shelbourne Hotel, and scanned every direction, but there were no members of the police force in sight. He wondered quickly if he should go into the hotel and ask them to phone for one, or run round the couple of streets to the government buildings at Leinster House where there were always one or two policemen on guard. But he was sure there would be too many explanations and delays in both cases, so he set off in the direction of Niall and the suspect, desperately hoping he would meet help on the way.

Then, about a hundred yards ahead of him, he saw a figure in dark blue with a peaked cap standing on the road beside the line of parked cars. He charged towards it, rehearsing in his mind what he was about to say, then stopped dead when he realised it wasn't a guard, but one of the unofficial car park attendants who hung around the area trying to con money out of unsuspecting drivers in search of a parking place.

'Blast!' Paudge muttered. He looked all round again, and wondered if he should turn back and head for the hotel. But then,

41

out of the corner of his eye, he saw Niall appear round the distant corner of the park railings. Instinctively, Paudge jumped between the parked cars and raced across the road, weaving dangerously through the traffic. Once on the other side, he walked as casually as he could in the direction of the oncoming Niall, hoping he would see him. He did. Niall loped across the road to him and they took advantage of the partial cover of a lamp post.

'That's him!' said Niall, directing a narrow-eyed hostile stare at a man who was walking slower than the other people on the opposite footpath. Niall took out the photograph from his jacket and held it in his hand for Paudge to see while he continued to monitor the man's movements. Paudge looked back and forward from the photo to the man on the other side of the street, but at that distance he could only shake his head and shrug his acceptance.

'If you say so ...'

'It's him all right. Just watch him.'

The suspect was sauntering along without direction or haste. Even though the sun was now burning in a tropical blue sky, he still wore a light raincoat, and had his hands deep in its pockets. There were four or five bicycles chained to the park railings, and another couple at parking meter posts, and the man looked at them all with careful scrutiny as he strolled past.

'He's got something under that coat,' said Niall as he and Paudge both turned their heads aside to avoid the man's attention. 'I bet you it's a boltcutter!'

The man had passed by opposite them, and the two boys began to drift along in the same direction on their side, trying to keep the other pedestrians between them and their suspect. Then the man wheeled around and began walking back. Niall and Paudge stopped with their backs turned to him before moving after him. But just as they did so, the man halted at a new-looking bike fastened to a parking meter post by a light steel cable and lock.

'Get down!' hissed Niall and he and Paudge sank to their knees behind a parked car. They got some odd looks from passers-by as they waddled like this to the gap between the cars to watch what the man was up to. He was looking up and down the footpath on his side, and occasionally across the road. A few people passed by him, but once there was nobody near, he bent down, opened his coat, and did something to the bike. A second later, he was up in the saddle and pedalling nonchalantly towards the corner Paudge had come from.

'After him!' ordered Niall, and he and Paudge sprinted away from their crouching position, almost knocking over two tiny nuns in the process.

'Are we going to grab him?' puffed Paudge as they weaved their way through the thin stream of people. The suspect was now on the road, but still pedalling with almost arrogant slowness.

'Looks like he's going left,' Niall answered. 'That'll take him past the guards outside Leinster House. We'll tell them and let them have the pleasure.'

Sure enough the man and the bike coasted lazily into the street on the left. But when the boys were about to round the corner just behind him, Niall pulled up sharply and shoved Paudge back out of sight behind the wall. The man had pulled up beside a very new-looking blue van, and dismounted. Another man in the driver's seat craned forward to look out of the passenger window as the suspect pulled open the sliding cargo door at the side and threw the bike in with a crash. Then he slipped into the front of the van, and it drove away down the street. Niall and Paudge emerged from cover and stared after it.

'Did you get the number?' Paudge suggested.

Niall half-turned, then suddenly leapt out into the roadway in front of a car that had just come round the corner. He pulled one of the doors open and stuffed Paudge into it, and it was only when Paudge had got himself back into an upright posture that he copped on they were in a taxi. Paudge was in the back seat and Niall was in front beside the driver, a silver-haired old man in a crumpled and besmudged grey suit. He was obviously bloated and stiff from years slumped at the driving wheel, and had to turn his whole body as he looked at them in anxious surprise.

'You're not going to mug me, are you?' he inquired politely. 'You're wasting your time if you are. I only just came on the road half an hour ago.'

'Follow that van!' Niall ordered with surprising authority. He pointed to the far end of the street where the blue van was halted at traffic lights, indicating a right turn. 'They just stole a bike. They stole my bike three weeks ago.'

The man stared at him for half a second, then slammed the gear lever forward and accelerated away so hard that the boys were thrown back in their seats. The lights had changed to green and the van went out of sight round the corner, but the old taxi driver flew after it like a formula one driver.

'Bike thieves, eh!' he chuckled as the taxi sailed round the corner at speed, sending Paudge over on his side and just missing a jay-walking pedestrian. 'You know I've been driving taxis in this town for nearly forty years, day and night, with bank robberies, and shootings and kidnappings all over the place, and not once did I ever get involved in any excitement. Forty boring law-abiding years, an' all the time I was just waitin' to get involved in a cops and robbers chase — probably saw too many Humphrey Bogart films when I was your age, huh?'

The taxi zoomed from lane to lane in the one-way system, bringing angry honks from the other cars and buses, and stares from the people on the footpaths. Paudge watched over the driver's shoulder, nervous but thrilled, as the blue van gradually drew nearer and nearer. They were on one of the main thoroughfares now, and the traffic was much heavier and slower-moving, but they managed to keep within half a dozen vehicles of their quarry, mainly by ignoring red lights.

'Sorry I thought you might've been muggers,' the old wizard at the wheel went on while the boys watched the blue van in tense silence. 'It's the biggest occupational hazard in this job, apart from piles. Most of the petty criminals in Dublin are under fifteen these days. Junkies most of them, too. I blame the parents so I do. Too soft.'

'He's turning right!' warned Niall, but the old man had already anticipated the move and swung across the road to follow, almost causing a pile-up behind them. As they roared into the narrow street Paudge noticed large 'No Entry' signs on either side, and big white arrows on the road pointing straight at them, indicating they were now going the wrong way down a one-way street. He was about to blurt out something to that effect before reminding himself that since the blue van had gone down it, they had no choice.

The van had stopped at the far end of the short, narrow street, and signalled a left turn. The taxi accelerated towards it and the driver lifted the microphone of his car radio.

'Once we can see his number I'll let the office know what's happening. They can get onto the guards to block him off a bit further on.'

Suddenly the taxi braked to a standstill, throwing all three of them forward. A lorry had emerged from a side lane right in front of them and completely blocked the road. The old taxi driver stuck his head and an arm out of the window.

'Get out of the way, eejit!'

The door of the lorry cab opened and a heavily-built man in a boiler suit jumped down, obviously fuming.

'Whadja mean eejit? This is a one-way street an' you're goin' the wrong way down it!'

The old taxi driver started to yell an explanation, but Niall pulled Paudge's arm and said, 'Come on.' They jumped out, leaving the taxi doors hanging open, and sprinted past the lorry and on down to the end of the street. They stopped at the corner and stared after the van, already far away on the road that ran along beside the wharves at the riverside, as it sped on to finally curve out of sight behind a warehouse.

Niall's shoulders sagged in dismay. 'Damn! Damn!'

'We can go to the guards. Did you get any of his number at all?' Paudge suggested once he got his breath back a bit.

Niall shook his head grimly. 'It's a waste of time. They're gone.' He turned and looked back up the street to where the old taxi driver and the big man in the boiler suit were still deep in heated conversation. 'Let's get the hell outa here,' he decided dismally.

★　　　　★　　　　★

Katy sat down at the desk in the corner of her bedroom once she had made up the bed and generally tidied up the place. She wanted to think out what she was going to do next, and being the kind of person she was, she just couldn't concentrate properly until everything was in its proper place. Not at all like her dad. He could work out the most impossible problems with a war going on around him. More like her mum in that respect: a calm, self-confident and quite attractive woman, who kept the household running quietly and smoothly, and almost seemed to be one step ahead of everything that happened and everybody's needs.

As these thoughts scrolled up the screen of her mind, Katy felt a sudden surprise at seeing her mother in this light, as if for the first time. She'd always known Mum was terrific, of course, but she'd kind of ... well, taken her for granted most of the time. It was strange to realise out of the blue that the woman in the kitchen was a real person, more than just Mum ...

And what's more, Katy's feverish brain circuits added a few microseconds later, before Mum was a mum she was undoubtedly a girl, and according to the laws of probability, had almost certainly gone through the very same things that Katy was going through right now. Maybe, some time in the distant past, she had felt the same way about Dad that Katy felt about Niall. Maybe she had even resorted to the same female trickery and low sexist ploys that Katy was about to stoop to. If so, she probably knew every warped thought and devious emotion now coursing through Katy's normally cool and ordered neural pathways ...

Enough of this paranoid nonsense!

Katy shook her head and cleared her mind-screen to receive new data. In front of her was the list of things requiring action that she'd drawn up with the aid of Fiona and Ruth. Some of the suggestions they'd made were outrageous, of course, but most of what they'd said was fascinating and extremely useful. They'd also given her a heap of old magazines wherein she could observe examples of the kind of things they'd been telling her about.

At the top of the list, Fiona had written, in enormous block capitals, CLOTHES!!! Katy turned to the pile of magazines and flicked through some of them, stopping at the pages which showed pictures of models in some extremely flamboyant ensembles, and feeling a great deal of anxiety at the thought of appearing in public looking like that. Not that she didn't want to. She did. It was just that she couldn't see how she could be noticed and admired without being stared at, which she detested.

'Don't worry about it!' Fiona had scoffed. 'Flaunt it! Make an exhibition of yourself! Once you've got over the first-night nerves, you'll get a kick out of making everybody look twice.'

Katy wondered. She stood up and looked at herself in the mirror. She had to admit Fiona had been dead right about her usual choice of colours: camouflage. Dull, drab, lifeless. No wonder so many buses almost ran over her on wet days.

She went to her wardrobe and looked inside. There wasn't a lot in it, and what there was consisted mainly of school uniforms, a sensible dress or two, and a variety of uninspiring odds and ends that she wore around the house.

'Right, then!' she told herself decisively. 'It's the Oxfam shop for this lot!'

She threw almost everything except the uniforms into a heap on her bed, then took out her Post Office savings book from a drawer in the dresser. She'd been saving half her pocket money and anything she got from relatives for birthdays and Christmas, with the intention of buying her own camera equipment so there would be no more problems over sharing Dad's when they went down the country. There was now £63 in the account. That'll do for a start, she thought.

Downstairs in the kitchen, she found some plastic bags and stuffed the clothes into them. Then she put on a jacket, checked she had her savings book and some cash, and headed for the door. On the way, she glanced at herself in the hall mirror and stopped. Those glasses. They made her look very large-headed and severe. She took them off and blinked as her eye muscles readjusted, then squinted critically at the slightly out-of-focus face in the mirror. Not bad. A definite improvement. But could she manage without them? Maybe it was time to try . . .

She opened the front door and there stood her mother with her friend Brid Ryan, both laden with boutique bags and parcels, looking worn out but satisfied, as they always did after a shopping expedition.

'Aaaaaah!' groaned her mother as she staggered into the hall. 'Tea! Quick! Before we expire! Have you got the kettle on, Katy?'

'Hello, Katy!' said Mrs Ryan, a squat oxo-cube of a woman whose pelican chin seemed to droop right down to her copious bosom. She let everything she was carrying plop onto the floor. 'Turned out a lovely day, didn't it? Whew! I'm hot!'

'I was just going out, Mum,' Katy explained. 'I have to do a bit of shopping.'

'Oh?' said her mother as she hauled off the raincoat that was stifling her. 'You should have said so earlier — you could have come with us.'

'This is something I have to do myself,' Katy informed her.

The tone of her voice made her mother look intently at her for a moment, then at the bags of old clothes she was carrying. The certainty that she knew everything washed over Katy again.

'Oh. I see. Well then. Off you go.'

Katy turned without a farewell and bounded down the four steps in front of the house.

'Katy!' called her mother, slightly alarmed. 'You've forgotten your glasses.'

'I didn't forget,' Katy told her. 'I deliberately left them off.' She turned away again, but after two steps turned back once again. 'But if I find I can't manage without them, d'you think we could afford to get me a set of contact lenses?'

5

Second Chance

'ARE YOU ABSOLUTELY one hundred per cent definitely positive it was him?' Paudge was on the point of breaking into a trot in order to keep up with Niall's angry lope.

'I told you, I've got Katy's picture with me. Look for yourself.'

Niall took the photo from his jacket and thrust it at Paudge without interrupting the rhythm of his stride. Paudge squinted at the image of a youngish man with greasy, blond hair that curled up over his collar.

'It looks a bit like him all right.'

'It IS him!' Niall snarled, and snatched the photo back. Paudge replied by slowing down to a stroll and letting a growing gap open up between them. Niall ignored this for a hundred yards, then stopped at a corner to let Paudge catch up.

'Sorry, Paudge,' he growled. 'It's just . . . we'll never get another chance to catch them. We had them right there!'

'We should go to the guards anyway,' suggested Paudge.

'Waste of time!' snapped Niall. 'They're only interested in bank robbers an' big-time stuff, not bicycles. Come on, let's go home.'

They had spent half an hour scouring the city centre streets in the hope that the villain's van might still be in the vicinity, and now found themselves standing near the stately Post Office building on the wide thoroughfare of O'Connell Street, so they crossed over and headed silently and glumly towards Connolly Station, the main station that lay about a mile away towards the docks area.

'Hang on,' said Paudge after they had traversed about half a mile, and he disappeared into a shop. He reappeared clutching chocolate bars in one hand and a brown paper bag in the other.

'Have this,' he urged Niall in a tone of condolence, and handed him the chocolate bars. Niall took them with a grimace indicating thanks, and Paudge produced a banana from the bag. They ate and walked at a more leisurely pace for a while.

'At least,' Paudge mumbled through a mouthful of masticated banana, 'we proved old Four-Eyes' walkie-talkies work great, eh?'

He pattted the apparatus strapped to his middle and looked to Niall for agreement. But Niall suddenly leapt at him and squashed him flat against the wall behind them.

'Shut up! It's them!' Niall spat out before Paudge could cough enough of the banana out of his gullet to allow him to protest.

They had just been about to cross a gap in the buildings through which ran a cobbled lane. Niall slithered to the corner of the wall and looked round it with one eye, and then beckoned Paudge to do

49

likewise. The lane went straight between the buildings for about thirty yards, then turned right to run parallel to a high, stone viaduct that carried the railway lines across the central part of the city. The arches under the viaduct were closed off to form storehouses or sheds, and in front of the open door of one of these sheds stood a blue van and a youngish man with greasy blond hair.

'It's them!' Paudge agreed as they both pulled back quickly from the corner and stood with their backs tight against the wall, eyes wide and hearts thumping. Across the road, a scruffy band of small children had stopped to watch them with amused curiosity.

'Run for the guards!' Paudge blurted, and he was almost gone when Niall grabbed his jacket.

'We'll do it right this time,' said Niall. 'Go back to the pub on that last corner and phone them from there. Hurry!'

Paudge needed no telling and was gone in a flash. The scruffy kids drifted on, disappointed that there wasn't going to be a fight as they had hoped.

Niall crept back to the corner and put his eye round. The van was still there and the shed still open but the blond man was gone. Then another man, squat and dark and dressed in jeans, came out of the shed, pushing a bicycle. He went out of sight at the side of the van for a moment, then went back into the shed emptyhanded. The blond man came out with another bicycle and did the same. Then the dark man again. Niall counted seven bicycles, and then they stopped. He looked round tensely for Paudge, but there was no sign of him returning yet with good news, no wail of police sirens approaching at speed. The men were still inside the shed. Niall decided to risk moving in closer to get the number of the van in case they slipped off again before help arrived.

He psyched himself up for a moment, then sprinted flat-out between the buildings, hoping there would be something he could hide behind once he had cleared the dark brick walls of the rear yards. There wasn't. On either side were vacant areas of bare soil, churned up where the users of the sheds parked their vehicles. The only object around was the blue van itself, so he kept on going, running on his toes so as to make as little noise as possible, till he reached the side of the van facing away from the open shed door.

He pressed himself up against it, making sure his legs were behind the rear wheel and out of sight to anyone on the other side. He listened, fighting to keep his gasping breath as quiet as possible. Through the pounding pulse in his ears, he could hear the two men talking inside the shed.

'We'll leave these two,' one was saying. 'They're wrecked with rust.'

'We'll leave nothing,' the other answered sharply. 'This place has to be clean. No evidence. We'll take them with us and dump them out at the other place. Okay?'

'Okay, okay!'

Niall froze and held his breath as he heard the men come out of the shed and pile two more bikes into the van through the side door. He tensed himself for another top-speed sprint back up the lane if either of them started to walk round.

'Right,' said the second voice. 'Now we'll just have a last look around to make sure we haven't left anything by way of evidence behind us.'

'Aw, come on: you've been watching too many TV cop shows. Let's go.'

'Listen, Doyler, you haven't done time inside. I have, an' I want to make sure I don't do any more. That's why I'm careful. Come on.'

The two men went back inside the shed, and Niall could hear the first one grumbling and complaining amid noises of things being moved and kicked around. He slid along the van's side to the driver's window and looked in, but the driver's cab was sealed off from the cargo section, so he could see nothing. He slipped back to the other end and slithered carefully round to the back doors. The door of the shed hid him from the two men inside, so he carefully eased open one of the van's double rear doors and squinted in. Immediately in front of him were a couple of small tea chests filled with bits of bikes, a heap of bicycle wheels, and a crumpled up tarpaulin cover. Behind these, the rest of the van was crammed with bicycles of every variety and condition.

'Wow!' whispered Niall. 'They must be moving out.'

He closed the door again silently, and listened. The men in the

51

shed were still working and talking, but he knew they would stop soon and then come out to drive away. He looked anxiously up the lane to the empty gap between the buildings.

'Come on, Paudge! Hurry up, will you!' he prayed.

*   *   *

Paudge, meanwhile, was having trouble. As instructed, he had galloped up to the pub at the corner, and burst in through the swing doors, wild-eyed and still clutching his bag of bananas. The pub was dim and deserted, except for two old men poring over the racing pages of a newspaper at the bar. They looked up at him, as did a bald-headed surly barman who was loading beer glasses into a dishwasher.

'Phone!' Paudge panted, out of breath. 'Where's the phone?'

One of the old men pointed to where a payphone hung on the wall beside a toilet door. Paudge charged over to it, seized the handset and began dialling 999, dropping his bananas in the process. The two old men and the barmen stared at him impassively. There was a click on the phone, then the ringing tone sounded twice before another click cut it off and made way for a buzzing drone. Paudge tried again, and the same thing happened. He was growing more agitated and anxious by the second, and an appalling stench from the partly-open toilet door was making him very angry. He dialled again, and this time someone answered:

'Emergency. Which service?'

'Guards! Get me the guards! Quick!'

'Emergency. Which service do you require?

'The guards!' Paudge repeated. 'I want the guards!'

The three men at the bar continued to stare.

'Hello? This is the emergency services number. Do you need help?'

'Yes!' yelled Paudge. 'I need the guards — and fast!'

But before he had finished speaking, the voice was already saying: 'Hello? Hello? I can't hear you. Can you ring on another line, please.'

Then a click brought back the buzzing drone.

'I can't get through!' he appealed to the three men at the bar.

'It's broken,' the barman informed him drily. 'Somebody stole the works out of the mouthpiece yesterday. We're waiting for the phone people to come and fix it.'

'But I need to get the guards!' spluttered Paudge.

'What's yer problem?' asked one of the old men, looking over a pair of tiny spectacles.

'It's my friend ... we saw this guy ... look, I can't explain — where can I get the guards?'

'Try running over to Store Street garda station, it's only a few minutes away down the road,' advised the barman disinterestedly.

Paudge flew out of the door, leaving his parcel of bananas behind him. The three men watched him go, then looked at each other and shrugged.

'World's gone mad,' muttered one old man, and turned back to the familiar uncertainties of the racing page.

Paudge flew down the street not really knowing where he was going. He was in a state of total panic by now. He raced several hundred yards, weaving through the weekend shoppers and strollers, before it dawned on him that he didn't know exactly where the garda station was. Somewhere near the river, wasn't it? He veered in that dirction and swooped round a corner, straight into the lower half of the most gigantic policeman he'd ever seen.

'Come with me, quick!' Paudge blurted without taking the time to be surprised. 'We've found them!'

'Found who?' The tall policeman let got of Paudge's shoulders which he had instinctively grabbed at the moment of impact. Paudge had to throw his head right back to look up at the youthful face perched on top of the towering uniform.

'Bike thieves! They stole my pal's bike! We saw one taking another one and followed them to their hide-out!'

Two tight lines formed between the tall policeman's eyebrows as he took this in.

'Bike thieves?'

'Yes! Now come on quick or we'll lose them again!'

Paudge grabbed the policeman's sleeve and hauled him as fast as he could in the direction of the laneway where he had left Niall.

Normally Paudge felt acute awe, if not downright fear, in the presence of an officer of the law. The very sight of one in the distance could fill him with nameless guilt, even though he might have done nothing more criminal that day than pick his nose and wipe it on the seat of his jeans. But the tension of the moment had given him unthinkable courage and such determination in his actions that the young garda allowed himself to be towed along without protest.

Retracing Paudge's route took them quite a few minutes and drew amused glances from virtually everyone they passed. Paudge was doing his best to accelerate, but the policeman, looking a bit like a circus stiltwalker with his huge boots swinging along on the ends of enormous legs, was unable or unwilling to work up any appreciable speed.

'This is it! Stay out of sight!' Paudge warned when they finally reached the laneway entrance. Paudge put his back to the wall and slithered towards the corner to look round. The policeman took his hat off, stood over Paudge, and leaned forward to do likewise.

The van was gone.

Paudge sprinted down the lane towards the shed the thieves had been working in, and the policeman stiltwalked after him. The shed door was shut, but when Paudge tried the handle, he found it was unlocked.

'Maybe they're inside!' he whispered urgently as the policeman strode up to him.

Together, they pulled the door suddenly open to reveal a dim and musty emptiness.

Paudge was dumbfounded. 'But ... they were here just ten minutes ago!'

'Well, there's definitely nobody here now, is there?' the policeman commented as he walked slowly round inside the bare shed. There was a rickety old bench against the filth-encrusted wall at the back, and dozens of flattened cigarette butts on the black, grimy floor. But apart from that, nothing.

'And where's this friend of yours, eh?'

'Niall!' Paudge looked around wildly. 'He's gone too!'

A train thundered past on the viaduct overhead.

'I think you'd better tell me the whole story,' said the policeman as he took out his notebook, a hint of scepticism in his eye.

Paudge rattled off the whole tale in barely two breaths.

'So you didn't actually follow that van all the way here? You just spotted it again.'

Paudge nodded.

'And since you didn't get the number the first time, it might not have been the same van at all, just one similar?'

Paudge looked up at him, unable to say anything. He felt completely confused and drained, and his natural nervousness of the blue uniform was reasserting itself.

The policeman closed his notebook and let out a deep breath.

'Well, then. Maybe what's happened is that your friend realised it wasn't the same men after all when he got a closer look at them leaving and now he's gone off looking for you, or maybe even gone home. Eh?'

Paudge continued to stare silently up at him, which seemed to make the policeman grow uncomfortable.

'Look, you give me your name and address and then go and see if you can find your friend. Even if what you just told me is true, there's not a lot I can do about it without more information. Bring him round to the station and we'll see what he has to say. Okay?'

Paudge's insides were surging with half a dozen different feelings, uppermost of which was a perfect horror of giving a garda his name and address. So he invented one and gave him that.

The policeman shut his notebook and put it back in his pocket with a certain finality.

'Right then, Brendan. You go and track down this mate of yours, and we'll hear from you both later. But I'm fairly sure he's going to tell you it was a false alarm when you do find him.'

He swung the shed door shut and stiltwalked back up the lane with his arm on Paudge's shoulder. When they reached the street, he said, 'Good luck for now!' and headed back the way they had come.

Paudge stood in the entrance to the lane and looked back to where the van had been. He felt bewildered and helpless, but absolutely certain something serious had happened.

'Niall!' he muttered out loud, 'what've you done now?'

55

6

The Hideout

NIALL WAS ASKING HIMSELF the same question at that very moment.

He was lying in the back of the blue van, curled up and hidden under the tarpaulin cover at the back door. The van was being driven at a brisk speed through the city, and he was bumped and rolled back and forward and sideways across the small space he was occupying as it swung round corners or braked hard at traffic lights.

He had hung on till the last second, waiting for Paudge to reappear with help, but when he heard the two men agreeing it was time for them to get in the van and disappear, a surge of kamikaze determination took him quickly and quietly through the back door and under the tarpaulin before they re-emerged from the shed.

Only gradually did fear of what might be going to happen force its way through the anger that had pushed him to the point of recklessness. A wave of fright rolled slowly upwards from inside him, washed over the top of him, then rolled away into the psychological distance, leaving him covered in a cooling sweat from head to foot.

He could hear the two men talking up-front. It was a high-roofed van, the kind where the driver's cabin is separate from the cargo area, and the voices were muffled and barely audible above the drone of the engine. But as the minutes roared by, it was obvious they had no idea they had a stowaway on board, and Niall's confidence began to creep slowly back.

He checked if the back door of the van opened from inside and it did. With a clear escape route, he even began to feel some pleasant excitement about the situation. He checked the time on his watch, and then settled down to observe the route they were taking, holding the back door open just a fraction so as not to let in too much of the thick diesel exhaust fumes.

It became clear after twenty minutes or so that they were not heading for a destination in the city, but out of it. They sped through suburbs Niall didn't recognise, and gradually patches of fields began to appear between the housing estates and the houses themselves. The road seemed to be rising all the time, and at several points Niall caught a view of the receding city spread out behind and below him.

They must be heading into the Wicklow mountains, he thought.

This altered the picture yet again, and his anxiety returned. And it was too late to shout Geronimo and jump — clear of traffic lights and traffic, the van was roaring along tree-lined roads at a speed that had its jumbled cargo of bikes clattering around inside.

Up and up it went, the terrain changing all the time. Close-cropped fields were replaced by more unkempt land enclosed by crude stone walls instead of fences. Then cliffs of huge pine trees began to close in on the road, till eventually the van seemed to be roaring like a rocket through a dark, green tunnel, broken now and then by dazzling intervals of fierce sunlight.

Some signposts zipped past too quickly for Niall to read. Crossroads came and went, left turns, right turns. The thundering din inside the shell of the van began to give him a headache, and he felt as though he'd been crouching painfully on the cold steel floor for hours and hours, even though his watch said it was in fact only about seventy minutes or so.

The van rocketed along another forest tunnel, still dank from the morning's rain, and then lurched left onto an unsurfaced boreen. The bumps and potholes made the bikes behind Niall almost fall over on top of him, and he had to push hard against them with his free arm, which made his position excruciatingly uncomfortable.

Through the gap in the back doors, he watched about a mile of the tight overgrown laneway unwind from under the van's back wheels, twisting and turning through bleak boggy land and outposts of forest that were mixed and scruffy in comparison to the earlier neat and regimented rows of spruce.

Suddenly they were in a broken-down little farmyard. Small stone huts with rusty tin roofs appeared on either side, walls with faded and mud-spattered white paint, and one or two ancient bits of farm machinery crumbling away in thick beds of nettles. Without waiting to think, Niall exploded from the back of the van, sailed over a wall, and buried himself in the undergrowth of a thicket of bushes, all in the space of three seconds.

The van halted in front of a long low cottage with a corrugated iron roof covered in flaking red paint. Both men got out, and the short thick one went round to the back of the van.

'Doyler, ya eejit! Ya left the back door open!'

'I did not. I wasn't anywhere near it all day.'

The fat man looked inside the van while Doyler lit a cigarette and slicked back his greasy blond hair with a comb from the back pocket of his jeans.

'Don't think we lost anything,' the fat man shrugged. 'But we might have. Be more careful, will ya!'

Doyler was indignant. 'I told ya, I didn't go near ...'

'Hey! Did ya bring me drink!' The roar came from a muscular-looking man with flaming orange hair and beard who emerged from a shed on the other side of the yard. He wore a dirty boiler suit and his hands were black with oil stains. An enormous, curving black pipe protruded from the whiskers that hid his mouth.

'Ah, keep yer hair on PJ, it's on the front seat!' the fat man told him.

PJ found the brown paper parcel, pulled out and opened a bottle of beer with a bottle opener from one of his pockets, and sucked gratefully at the contents.

'Jaysus, I was needin' that. Howdja get on anyway? Everything cleared out?'

'It's all there,' Doyler said.

PJ looked in at the bikes, and seemed pleased.

'Some good ones in that lot. Yer learnin', Doyler!'

Doyler scowled and smoked.

'How're you fixed?' the fat man asked PJ, who sucked the last of the beer from the bottle and pointed with his thumb back to the shed he had come from.

'All finished and ready to go. You takin' them up to Belfast tonight?'

'Paddy Magennis down in Limerick says he's got clients. I'll take a load down there tomorrow first off. Belfast can wait. Did you make the dinner yet?'

'I was waitin' for Doyler here to come an' peel the spuds,' he grinned.

'I'm peelin' no spuds!' snapped Doyler.

PJ gathered up his parcel of beer from the van seat and headed cheerfully towards the cottage door.

'Well, the way it is with dinners around here, Doyler, them that cooks them, eats them. Them that don't go hungry.'

The three men trooped in through the dark doorway, Doyler leaving a long plume of smoke hanging in the air above it.

Under the bushes, Niall relaxed and took a deep breath. He could see the house and the van through a gap in the wall where once a gate had been, but reckoned he was out of sight to anyone looking out through the two tiny windows in the front of the house. He wriggled away from the gap till the doorway was hidden from him by the wall, then stood up in a low crouch and picked his way along beside the moss-covered stones till he was back at the entrance to the yard.

Like all such little settlements there was nothing anywhere to indicate any name or any other clue that might help to identify it. Niall's immediate instinct was to set off back down the road — not on it, but beside it on the other side of the wall, just in case — and hope he could stop a passing car when he eventually reached the main road. But then he looked up and saw a telegraph pole carrying two wires up to the house. A telephone. If he could get to it, he could dial 999 and get them to trace the line, then just sit and wait for the cops to come storming in and catch the trio red-handed.

He hopped across the muddy road in two steps, and jogged along behind the wall on the other side, still crouching low. The wall circled the yard, and part of it was formed by the side of the shed from which the orange-headed man had come. A tiny dirt-encrusted window allowed Niall to peer in. He could make out the shapes of bikes, but not much else. Maybe his own bike was in there? The thought gave him renewed determination.

He vaulted over the wall and crept along the gable end of the shed, all the time hidden from view of the house. He peered cautiously round to make sure the men were still inside, then skipped in through the shed door, heart thumping.

Inside was a veritable bicycle factory.

Bikes of every size and type stood in neat rows, gleaming and polished. Down one side was a bench, covered in tools and bits of bikes, and round it were bikes in various stages of dismantlement and reassembly. There was even a paint sprayer and tins of various colours of paint neatly ranged on a shelf. One or two freshly painted frames hung from the open rafters by wires, drying.

Jeepers, Niall muttered softly to himself. They've really got it organised.

He started looking among the rows of machines for his own racer, but there were so many he realised it would be a major operation to find it, so he went back to the door. The men were still inside the house. He skipped back round the corner and over the wall, and continued working his way carefully towards the cottage till he came level with a window at the back. Over the wall he slithered, ignoring the knocks from the rough stones, and crept up to the opening. He could hear pots and plates clattering inside, and the rich, jovial voice of the one called PJ.

'The trouble with you, Doyler, is you've nothing but mince inside yer skull. Ya must've been off somewhere complainin' about yer face when they were handin' out the brains!'

Niall found himself grinning as Doyler's voice retorted with a string of impotent oaths. His hostility towards Doyler and the fat one was absolute, but he was surprised to find he had a curious positive feeling about the big PJ. He'd always thought all criminals were bad news, but this one looked and sounded like he was good fun.

He slid round the side of the house to see where the phone wires entered the building, hoping the phone itself might be nearby. The two wires ended on a pair of heavy insulators bolted to the wall, and a smaller cable led down and in through a window. He peered in and there was the phone, right in front of him on a dresser. So far, so good.

He slipped round the house again and vaulted like a cat over the wall. He knew he would have to wait till all three men were out of the house at the same time, and since they were only sitting down to eat, that might take some time. So he picked a comfortable spot in the undergrowth among the bushes that inhabited the scrubby land between the farmyard and the forest, and sat down to wait, lifting his head to peer over the wall occasionally, absently chewing on stalks of grass.

He remained like this for about twenty minutes, his mind drained of everything except watching and waiting, when for no reason at all a huge idea leapt in front of his finely-concentrated attention: the walkie-talkie!

He unclipped it from his belt, checked that the power pack connection was still intact, held it up close to his face, and pressed the transmit button.

'Niall calling Paudge! Niall calling Paudge!' He was careful to keep the volume of his voice down to a forceful whisper. 'Do you read me? Over?'

He had always wondered about that term 'read' used by radio operators. It should obviously be 'hear', he was convinced. But 'read' was what everybody on film and TV always said, so he followed the incantation faithfully lest the magic should fail to work for him.

But fail it did. Despite the powerful energies inside him willing Paudge's voice to reply: 'Reading you loud and clear. Over!', all that came out of the little loudspeaker was a faint, dismaying hiss.

He tried again, this time turning up the volume.

'Niall calling Paudge! Niall calling Paudge! Do you read me! Come in please!'

That was another strange expression: 'come in'. Come in where? How?

The walkie-talkie only rasped unpleasantly in reply to the whispered pleas and the wondered questions.

Damn it, thought Niall. It probably hasn't occurred to Paudge to try listening on his unit. Even if he does, we could be listening and sending at different times. And then again, we're probably outside the range of the things now.

He felt like throwing the walkie-talkie away in irritation. So much for Professor Katy's bullshit. But after a moment's clearmindedness, he decided he would lose nothing by trying to call Paudge every five minutes or so till he could get to that phone in the house. He might just be lucky.

He was just about to try once more when two big, expensive-looking cars sped noisily into the farmyard and pulled up sharply at the house. Their startling arrival froze him into immobility for a few seconds till the men inside the cars threw the doors open and hauled themselves out. Wide-eyed and open mouthed, Niall shrank down to the cool damp earth.

They were all carrying guns.

★   ★   ★

Katy's head was spinning when she got off the train after her whirlwind shopping trip. Just as well she'd bought a return ticket at the outset, she'd spent every penny she had, except the last few coppers, which in a fit of giddy generosity she had tossed into the grubby hand of a filthy man obviously begging for his next drink. And good luck to him, she was surprised to find herself thinking.

She was delighted with herself and her purchases, neatly folded in four different boutique bags. Mummy would go mad when she saw what was in them, but that was a storm she would weather later. First she was just aching to get up to her room and try everything on together.

The result was probably going to be a shock even to her, she was sure. There was no sensible quality or discreet taste in this ensemble. It was all cheap, flash and flimsy, a basis of black partnered with lurid lemons and painful pinks, and everything with an exaggerated cut to it. Flamboyant, garish even. Great!

Hurrying up the hill from the station, she caught sight of the blond heads of the twins bobbing along behind a hedge in the street that led to Niall's place. Her lips thinned into nothingness and a knot of naked hostility formed between her eyebrows as they rounded the corner and saw her approaching. They nudged each other and exchanged little sniggering glances as she stepped off the pavement to give them as wide a berth as possible.

'Hello, mastermind!' jeered one of them. She still didn't know which one was which. 'Been shopping for some new encyclopaedias, have we?'

The twins chortled at this weak sally, but Katy only gave them a withering look and walked on in silence.

'Have you seen Niall anywhere today?' the second one called after her.

Katy stopped. Cousin Fiona's stern injunction to deal mercilessly with the opposition burned across her mindscreen. Then a totally new feeling, a gush of malicious intent galvanised her nervous system, and she turned to face them with a perfectly faked look of horrified astonishment.

'You mean you haven't heard?'

They shook their heads, smiles fading.

'He fell out of a tree this morning and broke his leg.'

They gasped in united horror and clutched at each other.

'Omagod! Is he badly hurt?!' they both demanded fearfully.

Katy savoured the dramatic effect of her first deliberate venture into the realms of untruth. Gone were the twins' cocky sneers, their arrogant self-assurance. They were at her mercy now and she exulted inwardly at the new sensation of power.

'He broke his leg,' she repeated. 'That's bad enough, isn't it?'

The twins gaped open-mouthed into each other's eyes.

'Is he in hospital? Which hospital is he in?!'

'Loughlinstown,' Katy lied coolly. 'You should go and see him. I'm going myself later.'

The twins looked helplessly at each other again, then turned and galloped off downhill without another word.

Katy watched till they were out of sight. Then she did a little dance of victorious delight on the spot, accompanying herself with squeals and yips, until somebody looked out from behind the curtains of a house on the other side of the street. She hurried off towards home, blazing with energy. That was those two taken care of. Now she had to get herself ready to track down Niall.

7

The Hostage

NIALL WAS DOING HIS UTMOST to make sure that nobody could track him down.

When the first shock of seeing the guns had begun to fade into ordinary fear, he slithered backwards into deeper cover under the bushes and lay there, heart drumming among his ribs. Then he heard big PJ's rich voice roll over the wall.

'In the name a' God, Gaskin, what the hell's all this for?'

An unpleasant laugh, high-pitched and fast as a machine gun, rattled around the farmyard.

'Don't worry, PJ old son, we didn't come out here to shoot you up!' sneered the laughing voice, thin but with an edge that hinted that its owner was dangerous and easily provoked. 'Me an' the lads just popped in for a social call, that's all.'

'Social, my arse. You're in bother, Gaskin, and by the look of it it's big bother this time. So just get back in them cars an' get the hell outa here, quick. Whatever it is, we don't want to get caught up in it.'

'Now that's not very sociable, PJ,' drawled the sneering voice, 'especially from somebody who owes me a favour, eh?'

'What d'ya want from us? Our business isn't of any interest to madmen like youse!'

'Easy now, PJ,' the voice warned slowly, 'let's not get insulting. All we're lookin' for is a bit of hospitality for a day or two.'

'Youse pulled a job an' now you need somewhere to keep outa sight till things cool off — that's what ya mean.'

'It's a bit more complicated than that, old son, but nothing for you to get excited about. If you'd just be civil enough to ask us inside, and give us a bite to eat and a couple a' drinks to steady the lads' nerves a bit, all will be revealed to you in due course.'

'Look, just turn round an' get outa here, will ya!'

'Sorry, PJ. We've no choice, an' neither have you. Now where's the grub?'

There was a short silence, then indistinct footsteps. Niall lifted his upper half to try to get a glimpse over the wall, but ducked down immediately when he saw a grim-looking, black-haired man, dressed in combat jacket and jeans and carrying a heavy-looking shotgun, crunch across the yard to the entrance. There the man took up a sentry position, slouching against the wall as he lit a cigarette and watched the muddy road with narrow eyes.

Niall slithered noiselessly backwards till the farm buildings and the man were completely obscured by the rustling bushes. Then he stood up and scuttled low through the undergrowth till he found a little clearing that was tightly surrounded by waving stems and leaves. There he quickly unbuckled his belt, pulled down his jeans, and squatted down to empty his bowels urgently.

That done, he felt a lot better. He stretched and shook his legs to get the stiffness of hours of crouching out of them, then, as the flies began gathering, scuttled off to find another well-hidden spot where he could consider the new situation.

Now that the gun gang had arrived, there was no chance of getting to the phone. That left the first two possibilities: contact Paudge on the walkie-talkie, or set off back to the main road and stop a passing car.

He tried the walkie-talkie again.

'Calling Paudge! Hello, Paudge! Niall calling! Come in, will you!'

No answer, only the dismal hiss. And a second attempt produced the same non-result. That was that. Paudge, you're useless.

Niall put the walkie-talkie back on his belt. The afternoon was wearing on towards evening and the shadows were getting darker and cooler under the bushes. He didn't feel very happy about the prospect of trudging across the wild landscape with no absolute certainty of making contact with help, but that was now the only course left open to him.

He stood up and began walking, but after a dozen steps, swung round in a manoeuvre that would take him round the back of the farmhouse again. Curiosity had once more gained a slight upper hand over the instinct to flee.

Even more carefully than before, he wriggled and scuttled his way through the scrubby tangle to the wall behind the farmhouse, where he waited and listened for a minute or two before gliding over again. He crept up to the window where he had heard the voices the last time, and crouched under it. No sound came to his ears. With his innards in knots of tension, he gently slid upwards till his right eye was just clear of the bottom left corner of the window.

Inside was a grubby room that must have been the farmhouse kitchen in its better days. In one corner, beside a battered dresser, was an ancient gas cooker at which the greasy-haired Doyler was irritably attending to something in a black frying pan. The fat black-haired bike thief was pouring tea into mugs on the table, while PJ, arms folded, learned back against the dresser to survey the four men seated at the table as they hungrily demolished crude sandwiches consisting of whole sausages stuffed between slices of unbuttered white bread. The gang were fairly normal-looking types, dressed in jeans and combat jackets or anoraks, and without their guns, which they must have put down somewhere out of sight, didn't look all that villainous.

Except for one. He was smaller and thinner than the others, almost boyish. His hair was cut very short, a small, gold earring glinted in one earlobe, and even though the interior of the farmhouse was dim and gloomy, a pair of mirror-lens sunglasses covered his eyes. He was lolling back on a chair with one leg up on the table, drinking from one of PJ's recently acquired bottles of beer and cradling a heavy pistol in his lap. Slight though he was, there was something about him that communicated cold arrogance and danger.

All this Niall's eye absorbed in a few brief seconds before he shrank down again and sat with his back to the wall, listening, poised for instant flight.

'Good man, Doyler!' said a voice he hadn't heard before and which he assumed must be one of the hungry gang. 'That was badly needed, that was.'

'Give us a bottle there to wash the grease down,' demanded another.

'Well now, PJ,' began the thin voice that Niall knew could only belong to the one with the sunglasses, Gaskin. 'How's the bicycle business treating you these days?'

'Cut the bullshit, Gaskin!' PJ's voice growled back. 'Just tell us what kinda mess ye're in this time. What d'yez want here? What in the name a' all that's holy is all this artillery for?'

Niall could hear the hostile power in PJ's voice, the urge to lash out that was being held in check by the menacing presence of the guns. He could feel that PJ was just aching to grab the flimsy Gaskin by the throat and shake him senseless, the way a big black Labrador would with a rat.

Gaskin laughed. Probably he was caressing the heavy pistol in his lap, savouring the power it gave him over bigger men like PJ, who would otherwise dismiss him with a casual swipe.

'It's the big one this time, PJ. Something on a level way beyond you an' yer bicycle cowboys. Half a million greenbacks.'

'Half a million?' Doyler's voice echoed in amazement from the corner by the cooker.

'Beats your three hundred a week, eh Doyler?' Gaskin jeered.

'How?' PJ demanded. The monosyllable sounded like an order.

'Simple,' Gaskin replied after a few seconds' silence. Niall could picture them facing each other, PJ glaring into his own distorted reflection in Gaskin's mirror-lens glasses. 'We took a hostage. Rich foreigner. Boss of a big company. They pay up, he goes home.'

There was a tense silence.

'Gaskin,' came the voice of the fat black-haired bike thief, 'ye've really done it this time. Flipped out completely. Ye'll do thirty years when they get you, an' I'm not waitin' around to get caught in the middle when they do come after youse!'

'Stay where you are, O'Brien!' Gaskin ordered curtly. 'Nobody does anythin' I don't tell them to. Right?'

Niall knew Gaskin must be waving his gun around like a bad cowboy in a black-and-white B movie.

'We don't want to be here any more than youse want us here,' Gaskin went on. 'We had another safe house lined up in town, but things didn't work out for us. The guards got in the way. So here we are, an' here we have to stay — youse an' all — till we figure out the next move.'

'Where is he?' PJ's voice had gone very cold.

'In the boot of the BMW,' Gaskin drawled disinterestedly. Then, 'Come back here, PJ!'

Sounds of hurried movement came through the window to Niall, triggering his own tensed muscles into action. He zipped silently back over the wall and scuttled for cover, checking that he hadn't been seen before snaking his way through the undergrowth to a position where he could see what was happening in the yard.

PJ was helping a man out of the open boot of the car nearest the house. Gaskin and one of the other gunmen had casually followed him out, and Doyler and O'Brien, the fat dark bike thief, had come to the door to watch.

The man in the boot — arms tied behind his back, surgical tape over his mouth, and a piece of cloth wrapped over his eyes — was hardly able to stand up on his own, and leaned heavily against PJ as one of his legs kept buckling under him.

'Ya would've suffocated him if ya'd left him in there any longer!' PJ snarled at Gaskin. 'Ya want to be done for murder as well as everythin' else?'

Gaskin shrugged and grinned. 'They've done away with hangin'.'

PJ started to help the man towards the house.

'No!' snapped Gaskin. 'Put him in one of the sheds!'

PJ stopped and gave him a hostile stare, but Gaskin waved his gun in a determined manner.

'There's a good reason,' Gaskin told him through an evil, false smile.

PJ turned the man towards the shed where the bicycles were stored, it being the only one of the ramshackle outbuildings that had an entire roof and a proper door. Niall could see the man properly now they were facing in his direction. He looked like he was somewhere in his mid-forties, balding slightly and greying at the temples. He was of average height, slim, and dressed in an old track suit and runners. Not at all what Niall imagined the boss of a big foreign company should look like.

PJ guided him into the shed and re-emerged after a minute or so, pulling the door after him.

'He's not in great form. I suppose you gave him a belt on the head,' PJ demanded.

Gaskin shrugged and smiled his false smile again.

'He seemed to think travelling in the boot was beneath him.'

'We'll be all right if he doesn't have concussion.'

'Well, you can play the doctor an' keep an eye on him if it worries you that much. He'll be all right.'

'You could at least let the man lie on one of the beds inside.'

'No,' Gaskin said firmly. 'I don't want him overhearing anythin' that might blow our cover.'

'What cover? What are ya on about now?'

'He thinks we're the Provos, an' so do the guards.'

At the cottage door, O'Brien covered his face with his hands. PJ nodded grimly.

'Brilliant, Gaskin, brilliant. Ye'll have both sides comin' at ya now.'

Gaskin merely smirked. 'As long as yer man's employers think we're the boys, they'll take us seriously and pay up. By the time they work out it was a con, we'll be off to the sunshine.'

PJ gazed at him, shaking his head gently.

'Ya always were a header, Gaskin, but this is just utter lunacy, even for you. Is it drugs that's turned yer brain into soup or what?'

Gaskin's forehead muscles contracted and he waved the heavy gun at PJ: 'Inside!'

PJ's shoulders rose aggressively, but he obeyed.

'Come on in an' have a bit a grub!' Gaskin shouted to the man on guard at the gateway. 'There won't nobody be comin' up that road. We're okay.'

They trooped in and shut the door. Niall waited and watched, his stomach beginning to growl with hunger. But now at least there was no indecision in his mind about what he should do next. He knew.

★   ★   ★

Paudge didn't.

He had taken the train home on the policeman's advice, opting for the moment for the hopeful belief that the officer's theory on Niall's whereabouts was correct. He wanted it to be true. The alternatives were just too hair-raising to contemplate head-on.

But when he got to Niall's house, there was no avoiding them any longer.

'Ah, he's probably gone playing football or something,' Niall's father suggested. He wasn't very interested. He and Mrs Quinn were getting ready to go out to some social occasion or other, and he stumbled here and there with his peculiar nerveless gait, collecting up his handkerchief and his cigarette lighter and other little items.

Mrs Quinn sailed past in dignified haste, looking and smelling even more elegant than usual. She was a tall handsome blond woman whose presence always made Paudge feel like a plastic garden gnome.

'Hello, Paudge.' She didn't even look at him as she spoke. 'Niall not with you?'

Paudge almost blurted out his story, but managed to beat it back into the pit of his stomach.

'No.'

'That boy!' She checked her face in the hall mirror before pulling a coat over her shoulders. 'Well, when you do find him, tell him I said he's to come home and have something to eat immediately. Will you, Paudge?'

Paudge nodded, and Mr and Mrs Quinn hurried out to their car, waving curtly to him as they drove off and left him white-faced on the garden path.

He had no idea what to do next or where to go, so he went home to his own mother, who was as keyed up with anxiety as he was.

'In the name of heaven, boy, where have you been all this time?' She was always worried about him, and afterwards she was always angry at him for making her worry.

'In town,' he muttered gruffly. There would be no point trying to tell her either, that was obvious.

'Come and have your dinner, then!'

He followed her into the steaming kitchen, and sat down at the table while she heaped the plate in front of him with potatoes and vegetables and rashers of bacon and sausages, and buttered two slices of thick white bread for him.

He was halfway through the first mouthful of sausage when he remembered his diet.

'What's wrong!' his mother squawked as he spat the offending matter back onto the plate and pushed it away.

'I just don't want it.'

She stared at him, aghast with offended disbelief.

'But you have to eat something! You've had nothing decent all day — you'll make yourself ill!'

Suddenly Paudge realised why he was 'Podge': his mother had been forcefeeding him all his life. All her anxieties had become focussed on his gullet, like a mother bird eternally stuffing everything she could find down the gawping throat of her offspring in fear of famine in the morning.

He stood up and looked at her across the table. They were the same height, he hadn't really noticed that till now.

'Sorry, Ma, I just don't want to eat like this any more. I'm too fat. I want to lose some weight. I want to get a racing bike.'

'But you have to eat something . . .' she insisted.

He took an orange, a couple of apples, and a banana from the fruit bowl. His belly was roaring for its daily quota of sausages and spuds, but Paudge knew this was an important moment for him, and his stomach was on his mother's side.

'This'll do grand. I have to go out now. I'll see you later.'

His mother sucked in a sharp breath to fuel another outburst of protest, but he was gone before she could organise the words in her mouth, leaving her glaring in astonished dismay at the steaming heap on his plate.

In the soft air of early evening, Paudge proudly devoured the fruits of victory as he headed towards the home of the only person who might know what to do in the circumstances: Katy.

*   *   *

Niall made his move immediately the men went into the cottage and shut the door behind them. If he waited, he reasoned, they might be on their way back out again when he eventually chose to move.

He slithered over the wall beside the shed where they had put the hostage, and skipped round the corner to the door.

It was unlocked. Good old PJ.

Niall nipped inside and shut the door quietly behind him. At first he could see nothing in the gloom except the dull glint from handlebars and wheel rims. But then there was a shifting movement in a corner by the workbench, and Niall saw the white stripe that was the man's taped mouth. He stepped quickly over to him. The man's dark, anxious eyes looked up and registered an instant mixture of surprise and hope.

'Stand up and I'll untie your arms,' Niall told him in a whisper.

The man struggled awkwardly to his feet with Niall's help, and the rope was off him in seconds. He winced as he pulled the tape off his mouth, then let out a deep grateful breath.

'Thank you, thank you!' he whispered, sagging weakly against the bench for a moment. He pronounced the th almost like an s, but not quite as strongly as Germans do in films.

'We got to get out of here quick!' Niall told him urgently. 'Are you all right? Will you be able to do it?'

The man nodded.

'Yes, yes. Don't worry. I'm just painful from being in that kofferraum, the boot of the car. It will go away soon.'

Niall went back to the door and opened it a fraction, then hurried back.

'They'll probably be in there for a good while, unless PJ gets it into his head to bring you a cup of tea or something, so we'd better get going.'

The man rubbed his aching limbs, and looked around as his strength ebbed back.

'What is this place? Who are these people? Are you one of them?'

'No. I'm . . . Look, we don't have time for explanations. Let's go!'

'But how . . . Where are we anyway? We must contact the police.'

'We're in the middle of nowhere an' there's no police for miles and miles. Our only hope is to run an' keep running. Now, come on!'

He turned to lead the way out, but stopped _____

the door.

'Can you ride a bike?'

'Yes, but ...'

Niall immediately began extricating an i_____

machine with wide handlebars and a heavily spr_____

among the rows of bikes.

'You take this one,' he commanded. 'It's a moun_____ ___e. You

can go anywhere on that.'

The man obeyed silently, still dazed by what was happening to
him, and surprised by the coolness and control with which this
young boy was organising their escape.

'Pity there isn't another one for me,' muttered Niall as he hunted
around among the ranks of bicycles. Finally he pulled out a fairly
battered-looking BMX machine that was a couple of sizes too small
for him. He found a spanner on the bench and quickly pulled up
the seat post to raise the saddle.

'Now, listen,' he told the man. 'You go first. The entrance to the
farmyard is to your left. Get out as fast as you can — but for God's
sake, don't fall off!'

The man nodded and mounted the bike as Niall prepared to
open the door for his getaway. But when the door did open, the
man's mouth fell open and he sucked in a small gasp of air when he
saw what was outside.

'The cars!' he hissed. 'We could take one of the cars!'

Niall shut the door quickly, and they looked at each other for a
moment.

'But they could follow us in the other one.'

'If they have left the keys in them, we can drive one car and take
the keys of the other with us.'

Niall's coolness melted into its underlying fear. He knew that
meant he would have to go out there and check all three vehicles.

'All right,' he agreed after a moment's consideration, and
disappeared through the door.

He was back in barely thirty seconds, with one bunch of keys in
his hand.

'From the van,' he said. 'No keys in the others, but there's wires g from under the steering columns.'

Ah,' said the man. 'They have bypassed the ignition switches. They must be stolen vehicles.' He looked ridiculously disapproving.

'Anyway, that means they would follow us if we take a car, so it's out. Now let's get going, please!'

Niall swung the door open and the man mounted and wobbled through it. Then he pushed his little machine out and pulled the door closed behind him in case anyone should look out from the house once they had gone. Then he was flying down the bumpy boreen as fast as he could pedal. They were out. They had done it!

The two of them gasped and sweated along till they reached a junction where another boreen crossed theirs. The man braked and slowed, panting from unaccustomed exertion.

'Which way to the main road?' he asked.

Niall slowed to a halt in the middle of the muddy crossroads.

'We can't go that way. Once they find out you're gone, they'll be after us like rockets. They'd catch us in no time.'

The man considered this, blowing sweat off his upper lip.

'Yes, you are right. But what then do we do?'

Niall looked around. The road to the left led down and away across open bogland to distant rows of black gashes in the earth and little heaps of plastic bags that indicated a peat patch. To the right, the land rose through a scrubby wilderness towards the gloomy green of a pine forest behind which the sun was aiming itself for its eventual setting.

'Up there,' Niall said. 'That forest'll be full of tracks they could never take a car on. We'll lose them there.'

The man looked uphill and nodded. 'Good idea. Very good.'

They both turned their machines and rose on the pedals for the long upward slog.

*   *   *

Gaskin's lower jaw clicked from side to side, and the long barrel of the gun in his right hand betrayed a slight tremble.

'There's no way he could have untied himself. He was lashed at

74

the shoulders.'

He turned his burning eyes slowly up to PJ, while the other members of his entourage stood around in the gloom of the bicycle shed, arms hanging helplessly at their sides. Doyler and O'Brien observed cautiously at the doorway.

'Well, he must be Houdini, then,' PJ offered as an explanation. 'We was all inside with youse, you know that.'

'Yeah,' nodded Gaskin. 'But it was you who brought him in here. On yer own.'

PJ sucked in a slow breath that seemed to expand him to twice his size. 'You sayin' it was me that untied him?'

Gaskin stared at him, totally unintimidated by the pent-up physical power that was radiating through PJ's dirty boiler suit. 'Somebody must've.'

One of Gaskin's men took a step forward. 'Look, instead a' wastin' time arguin' about who done it an' how, why don't we just get after him before he gets too far?'

'An' how are we gonna track him down in that wilderness out there, eh?' Gaskin snapped.

PJ looked to the side, to where his previously neat rows of bicycles were now standing somewhat askew with an obvious gap in their ranks.

'He hasn't gone across the land. He took a bike. He's gone down the road.'

Gaskin's eyes changed suddenly.

'Right. Bring in them other two,' he ordered his men. 'Tie them up together. Tight.'

Doyler and O'Brien resisted only faintly as the gunmen pulled them inside and begin lashing them back to back with odd bits of rope, cord and wire that were lying about.

'You, my big friend,' Gaskin told PJ in a steely tone, 'can come with us for the ride.'

'Whadja need me for? I'm not gonna help yez.'

'It's like this, PJ old son. If we don't get him back, it won't be bicycles you'll be lookin' to rob, it'll be a wheelchair.'

He pointed his gun at PJ's knees. PJ started to say something, but clamped his jaw shut with an audible snap.

75

'Shove them two in a corner,' Gaskin ordered, 'an' let's get a move on.'

He attempted to give PJ a shove towards the door, but PJ's bulk was too much for his thin arms so he resorted to prodding him with the gun. PJ obeyed the unspoken order, but with a deliberate saunter. Gaskin guided him to one of the cars and made him get in the back seat. He climbed in beside him, keeping his gun pointed at him all the time, while one of his henchmen jumped into the driver's seat and the others piled into the second car.

The engines roared, but as the cars shot backwards to manoeuvre out of the yard, Gaskin suddenly shouted, 'Stop!'

He scrambled out and ran into the house, returning after a few seconds with the telephone in his hand, wires trailing behind him. He threw it in a high arc over the wall and it fell into the bushes with a thrashing sound.

Then he turned to the van, took aim with his gun in both hands, and put a bullet in each of the two front tyres and two through the radiator and into the front of the engine.

The noise of the shots echoed deafeningly among the farm buildings. Terrified birds fled shrieking from under the scrubby trees all around, and in the bicycle shed, Doyler and O'Brien yelled something indistinct. Water splashed from the punctured radiator.

'Just in case there's any more Houdinis around the place.' Gaskin grinned monkey-like at PJ as he got back into the car.

'Go!' he instructed the driver.

The two cars shot through the gateway and bounced down the boreen.

8

Contact!

KATY SAT in front of the dressing-table mirror in her bedroom, gazing in deep concentration into her own image as she oh so carefully and delicately applied the eye make-up the way she'd read in the magazine. By her side, a radio cassette player thrummed rhythmically, and the words 'She loves you, yeah yeah yeah!' reassured her at a pleasantly low volume. She'd tried bopping to the trite, trashy stuff on the pirate stations the way Cousin Fiona and friend Ruth did, but somehow she just couldn't make herself stoop that low. A line had to be drawn somewhere, and for her it came below The Beatles. Some of their later stuff was almost symphonic. Quite respectable, really.

She put down the little eye-brush and leaned back to take in the total effect of her artistry. It was stunning.

'Is that really me?' she wondered out loud as she turned her head from side to side, swivelling her eyes to keep them trained on the magically transformed face two feet in front of her.

Gone were the freckles that used to be dusted across the lower part of her forehead and the bridge of her nose. They were now cunningly hidden under an equally invisible new skin she had concocted from half a dozen tubes and little flat tins lying in front of her. And the shape of her face had changed too. The cheekbones were higher and more prominent, and the cheeks themselves less full, less childlike. Her lips had become a focus of this living painting and looked so inviting she nearly leaned forward to kiss them on the cold glass of the mirror. It was absolutely amazing. Astounding. That somebody like her could be so easily transformed into a creature so ... well, so attractive. So actually feminine. She'd always agreed with the feminist standpoint that the stereotyped image of the painted woman portrayed in the media was obscene. But now that she'd actually tried it for herself she had to admit it gave her a real buzz. Besides, she wasn't really doing it just for the ego trip, it was a tactical necessity. All's fair in love and war, even sexist obscenity.

'Katherine! There's somebody here to see you!'

She gasped at the sound of her mother's call from downstairs. She leapt to the locked door of her room and shouted through it with forced coolness.

'I'll be down in a moment!'

She leapt back to her seat and began scouring her face with

tissues soaked in something from a plastic bottle. The alluring new Katherine that had taken the best part of half an hour to create was scrubbed out in the space of a few seconds, and the familiar Katy re-emerged from underneath, red-cheeked from all the rubbing, and eyes bright with panic.

She forced herself to walk downstairs in a calm and moderate manner. Paudge was waiting in the hall, looking anxious and drawn.

'Oh,' she said, and stopped. 'It's you, Paudge.'

For no good reason other than that she wanted it so, she had been expecting Niall.

Paudge saw the surprise in her still-pink features and assumed the loss of weight from his crippling diet must already be visible to the world. He pulled up his chest and pulled in his belly.

'Katy,' he began, 'I've got to talk to you.'

She looked at him for a moment and her forehead muscles gathered.

'What is it?' she asked as she walked down the remaining steps and stood in front of him.

Paudge turned his eyes towards the open kitchen door, through which came the voices of Katy's mother and her friend, still letting off steam after their day in town. Katy understood that Paudge, for some reason, did not want them to overhear whatever it was he had to tell her. She started to turn round to lead him upstairs to her room, but then remembered the forbidden potions lying on her dressing table so she turned aside and ushered him instead into the empty sitting room.

There, his inner agitation bubbled up to the surface and he fumbled nervously in his pockets as he tried to get the words out, while Katy stood looking at him with increasingly puckered eyebrows. This, she could see, was something serious.

'It's about Niall,' he began reluctantly. He was still scared to let his own pent-up feelings come out, and resentful that he had had to bring them to someone that both he and she knew was a rival. And a girl at that, even if it was only old Brainbox.

'What about Niall?' Katy was beginning to pick up some of his apprehension.

Paudge looked her helplessly in the eyes.

'I think he's been murdered.'

Katy sat back on the arm of the settee with a thump.

'Murdered?' she echoed in a small voice.

She seemed on the point of falling over in a faint, and that made Paudge feel a bit better. At least he wasn't the weakest now.

'Well, he might just have been kidnapped. He could still be alive. I don't know for sure.'

The effect of his words on Katy was really giving him renewed strength now. She put her hands to her face and pulled her mouth open, her eyes wide with horror. Then she jumped towards the door.

'We have to do something! We've got to call the guards!'

Paudge grabbed the back of her sweater and reeled her in.

'I've done that already. They didn't believe me. Nobody believes me. They won't believe you either. You don't know what happened anyway.'

She plumped down on the arm of the settee again.

'What did happen?' she asked in a voice that indicated she'd almost rather not hear the reply.

Paudge let the whole story gush forth in one long sentence, dispensing with such unnecessaries as commas and full stops, simply linking it all together with a liberal sprinkling of 'and thens'. He ran over every little detail, starting with the train journey into town, the rain, the cinema, the walkie-talkies, the bike thief, the van, the chase in the taxi, losing the van, spotting the van again, running for the guards, the men in the pub, the enormous policeman, and finally the disappearance of van, bikes and everything, including Niall.

The only thing he omitted to mention was his diet. For personal reasons.

Katy listened to it all with lips parted, and said nothing for quite a few seconds after he had finished his tale and crashed backwards into an armchair, drained and exhausted.

'What about Niall's mum and dad? Did you tell them?' she finally asked.

Paudge nodded wearily. 'They've gone out somewhere. They

weren't very interested. He always gets home late anyway, so they won't start to worry till tomorrow morning when they realise he's not in bed. It'll be too late for poor Niall by then — too late to help him, I mean.'

Katy stood up, chewing her bottom lip. She smacked a fist into her palm.

'If only my dad was here — he'd know what to do. He's the only adult I know who isn't a total eejit!'

'When's he coming home?' Paudge inquired hopefully.

'He was called out on a job somewhere in town, some big firm's computer sat down. He could be gone a couple of hours or a couple of days, you never know.'

'Couldn't you get in touch with him?'

She shook her head impatiently. 'He goes off his nut if you disturb him at work. Anyway, he didn't tell us where he was going.'

Paudge sagged deeper into the chair, his features sinking downwards as if the flesh was turning to lead.

'What are we going to do?' he whined in despair, the helpless one again.

Katy ignored him and paced slowly across the room, eyes burning with mental energy as she fed the data into her subconscious computer and waited for the solution to appear line by line on her mindscreen.

She did not have to wait long.

'The walkie-talkies! Of course!'

She bounded across to Paudge in two steps.

'Where's yours? Has Niall still got his with him?'

'Yes, he has!' Paudge answered with a start as her intentions became clear to him. He hurriedly unzipped his jacket, unclipped the walkie-talkie and power pack from his belt, and handed them to her.

She took the set from him and looked at it with a frown.

'There's two problems. One, he might be well out of range, and two, he might not have the thing switched on at all.'

'I thought you said they could work up to thirty miles?' Paudge complained.

'They can, under optimum conditions.'

'What does that mean?'

'Well, both units would have to be operated up on a height — a hill or a high building — with no obstructions along the line of sight between the two points. Niall could be down inside a building, or lying in the back of that van you saw. He wouldn't hear anything then even if he was listening.'

'And we couldn't hear him if he was trying to contact us?'

She nodded grimly.

'So that's no use either!' Paudge said in despair.

Katy consulted her internal computer again.

'Listen,' she told Paudge seriously. 'It's a fair bet that if Niall is in trouble, he'll have the sense to try using the walkie-talkie to call for help. He's intelligent, and he doesn't get hysterical, like some people.'

Paudge sensed an implication in her words, but simply sucked his lips and nodded meek agreement.

'Now, we don't stand much chance of contacting him, or even hearing him with this,' she went on, holding up the walkie-talkie. 'But I think I know a way we can. Come on.'

She led him out of the room and up the stairs. They had just about reached the first landing when her mother popped her head out from the kitchen and looked up at them with some surprise.

'Paudge wants to borrow a couple of books on electronics,' Katy told her without hesitation. She seemed to have discovered a new aptitude for on-the-spot fabrications. 'He's thinking of taking it up himself.'

'Is he,' her mother said, more as a comment than a question, as she looked from one to the other and back again. Then she gave a small shrug and withdrew her head into the kitchen again.

'I know what she's thinking,' Katy muttered as she and Paudge went past her locked bedroom door and on up to the attic laboratory. Paudge's pale face turned slightly pink at the idea of coming under an adult's suspicion for that kind of thing.

Katy switched on the lights in the attic and went straight to the corner where the radio station was housed. She flicked switches and turned a few knobs before sitting down in the operator's chair.

'Now,' she began, and seemed about to explain things more to herself than to Paudge. 'The handsets operate on a frequency at the bottom end of the two-metre band, so if we tune the transceiver to the same spot, we'll have a far better chance of picking up Niall, and he'll have no problem hearing us. If he's listening.'

She stood the walkie-talkie on the bench beside her, switched it on, and tuned around on the dial of one of the impressive-looking pieces of equipment.

'Does that transceiver thing have more power than the walkie-talkies?' Paudge inquired. His fascination with the electronic gadgetry had almost made him forget how anxious he was.

'Tcha! There's no comparison!' Katy snorted. 'The walkie-talkies are only toys beside this thing. It's got an output of forty watts P-E-P.'

'What's P-E-P?'

'Peak envelope power.' She shook her head like a dog. 'Don't ask what that means, it's too complicated to explain right now.'

Paudge's next question was blown away by a high-pitched howl from the loudspeaker at the transceiver. He slapped his hands over his ears, but in the instant it took him to do so, the howl had dived through all the frequencies in between to a low, grating rumble and then out of the audible range altogether.

'That's it,' Katy announced. She switched off the walkie-talkie and did something with a couple of small knobs on the transceiver. 'We're locked onto Niall's frequency now.'

Paudge pulled a chair next to her and sat down, watching Katy's every move with rapt eyes.

'What do we do next?' he asked eagerly.

Katy took exception to his use of the word 'we', but decided under the circumstances to let it pass. She leaned forward to press another switch on a small metal box, and the thin line of light in the plastic map box on the wall, the antenna direction indicator the two boys had marvelled at the last time he had been in the attic, came on. It began in the centre of the distorted map of the world, in Dublin, and cut across the west of the country, out over the empty Atlantic, and then into the United States, from the north via Canada, because of the crazy angles at which the continents were lying.

'We'll make a few passes with the beam,' said Katy. She turned a knob on the transceiver and the loudspeaker began to hiss faintly. Then she threw another switch and the line of light on the map box began to move around, a slow ticking noise coming from it as it went.

'Every tick represents a ten-degree sweep of the antenna system outside,' Katy informed him, but he was staring hypnotised as the line of light crossed the North Pole, the Bering Straits, Siberia, China, Central Asia, ticking slowly along on its journey round the strange world of the map, a world with Ireland at its centre point.

'Do you really think Niall's been taken out of the country?' Paudge asked incredulously as the line crept on towards Russia and Europe.

Katy allowed herself a little snort of amusement.

'I'm only using the indicator to check the compass direction of the beam,' she told him. 'We're on a VHF band, and those signals wouldn't normally get out of the country, even with a high-power transmitter. I'm turning the antenna from west through north to east to sweep the city. We're south of it, you see.'

Paudge nodded agreement, lips hanging open. No point in appearing thick even if you don't really see.

Katy clicked some more switches in a businesslike manner.

'Nothing there. We'd better try calling him. He might be listening.'

She stopped the rotating light on the map box, and did something that made it start clicking in the reverse direction. Then she picked up a microphone that stood on the bench, cleared her throat, and held down a switch.

'Hello, Niall. Hello, Niall. This is Katy calling you. Hello, Niall. Can you hear me? Over.'

The loudspeaker hissed its low soft hiss, a sound that somehow made Paudge think of stars and galaxies and dark, cold, empty space. Weird.

'Hello, Niall. Hello, Niall. This is Katy calling. Can you hear me? Over.'

Katy kept repeating the message in calm, clear tones as the beam indicator ticked back and forth on the wall, but only the hiss came back in reply. Eventually, after nearly fifteen minutes of calling vainly for Niall to come in, she put the microphone down and let out a huff of frustration.

'If he was listening at all, he would have heard us by now. I think we might be wasting valuable time,' she said darkly.

'What'll we do, then?' Paudge wondered again.

The beam indicator on the wall ticked on, this time coming right round in a full sweep of the bottom part of the map. Katy reached out to switch it off.

'We have to go back to the guards and convince them to do something. I'll tell my mother. She'll help us.'

She flicked the beam indicator switch off. At that very instant, the hiss from the loudspeaker became louder and rougher, stayed like that for three or four seconds, then changed back to its original sound.

'What was that?' said Paudge, startled.

'Sssshh!!' Katy ordered as she grabbed the microphone and pushed down the transmit switch.

'Hello, Niall! Hello, Niall! This is Katy! Can you hear me? Over!'

At first there was only the usual tone from the loudspeaker, but the louder rough hiss came on again for several seconds before once more stopping abruptly.

'Is it him?! Is it Niall?!' Paudge gibbered excitedly, hanging over the bench to get nearer the loudspeaker.

Katy pushed him back onto his chair and pressed the transmit switch again.

'Hello, Niall. This is Katy. If that's you trying to call us back, we can't hear you very well. You're very faint. Have you got the booster pack connected? Over.'

Again the hiss changed for a few seconds, then changed back again. But there was no intelligible sound among the ssshhrasssh.

Katy switched on the beam indicator again and looked at the position of the stationary light bar. Paudge was jerking and twitching in his chair.

'Is it him? Is it Niall?' he persisted.

'I don't know,' she told him flatly, still considering the map. 'But if it is him, he's not in the city at all, he's somewhere southwest of us, in the Wicklow mountains.'

Paudge looked up at the map and the line of light, but he couldn't really see how she had worked that one out.

'Maybe he picked up our signal off the back of the antenna when we were transmitting in the opposite direction towards the city,' Katy thought aloud.

She turned abruptly to Paudge. 'Does Niall know the morse code?'

Paudge shook his head slowly. 'I don't think so.'

Katy picked up the microphone again.

'Hello, Niall. This is Katy again. Listen carefully: I can't pick you up on voice transmission. You must be too far away. But there's another way we might be able to do it. If you look at the walkie-talkie, you'll see a button marked CW. That works like a morse key. Now, what I want you to do is this: when I ask you a question, you press that button down quickly three times to make three dots for yes, or hold it down to make a long dash if it's no. Did you understand?'

She pressed another switch on the transceiver, and from the hissing loudspeaker came three short clear tones.

'It *is* Niall!' she exclaimed jubilantly, leaping up from her seat.

Paudge jumped up and nearly hugged her with delight and excitement.

'Tell him I'm all right!' he spluttered.

Katy disentangled herself forcibly from his octopus arms and pushed him back on his bum.

'Niall, this is Katy again!' she gushed into the microphone. 'We're picking you up now — not very strong, but dead clear. Now, can you answer these questions the same way. Are you okay?'

The clear dots came from among the loudspeaker's hiss.

'Great! Paudge's here with me, he told me all about the bike thieves and the van. Did they catch you? Are you being held captive?'

A long dash. Katy and Paudge looked at each other with a mixture of puzzlement and relief.

'Are you in danger?'

A pause, then three dots.

'Have you any idea where you are?'

Another long dash.

Katy looked up at the beam indicator and bit her lower lip thoughtfully.

'Listen, Niall: you're somewhere in the mountains along a line that runs south-west of here, but I can't pinpoint your position exactly. Can you estimate how far from the city you are?'

A long dash said no.

Katy looked at the microphone for several seconds, and Paudge realised she was running out of ideas for the moment. He snatched it from her and pressed the transmit switch.

'Niall! This is Paudge here! I got a guard, Niall, but he didn't believe me when we got there and the van was gone an' you too. What happened t'you? Did you hide inside the van or something?'

Three dots.

'Are they after you now?'

Three dots again. Katy grabbed back the microphone.

'Listen, Niall, we're going to talk to the guards again, they'll have to believe us now. Keep listening every ten minutes and we'll contact you as soon as we've done that. Can you hang on that long?'

Three dots. Katy and Paudge stood up together, both looking as though they were having difficulty taking in what was happening.

'I'll go tell my mother,' Katy said. 'We can't handle this on our own.'

But before they could get going, footsteps clumped up the stairs and the attic door swung open to admit a man who was the dead image of Katy, except for his orange beard and balding head.

'Hello there!' he said in surprise when he saw the pair standing at the radio station. He was carrying the entrails of some kind of electronic device in his hands.

'Dad!' Katy squealed as she rushed forward to greet him. 'Dad — Niall Quinn's in big trouble! He's somewhere out in the mountains and a gang of bicycle thieves are after him!'

'Eh?' He put down whatever it was he was carrying and looked from Katy to Paudge, nonplussed by the white seriousness of their faces.

Katy rapidly told him the story as she knew it, with help of a few explanatory footnotes from Paudge. Her father listened to it all in silence, the muscles on his naked scalp twitching now and then as the braincells underneath assessed the bizarre situation.

When Katy and Paudge had finished, he went on looking at them unspeaking for a few moments, then:

'Well, then. We'll certainly have to get the guards moving on this one. But we can't risk leaving it all up to them. We'll have to do something ourselves.'

'But what?' Katy pleaded, almost hopping with desperation.

Her father took off his crumpled tweed jacket and walked over to look at the light bar on the wall map.

'We can pinpoint Niall's exact position for them,' he said.

'But how?'

He was already rooting among the jumbled equipment on the shelves at the side of the room.

'Geometry,' he assured her without looking up. 'Simple geometry.'

9

On the Run

NIALL AND HIS COMPANION had kept going at the full limit of their abilities for more than half an hour before they felt it reasonably safe to stop and allow their heart rates to fall to more comfortable levels.

It had surprised Niall how well the man had managed to stay the pace. Obviously the track suit was not just a fashion accessory as it was with most adults of his age. The only problem he'd had, and it wasn't a serious one, was with the bike.

'I haven't sat on a bicycle since I was fifteen,' he confessed between gulps of air as they toiled their way up the last steep slope of the boreen and the silent forest closed protectively in on either side of them. 'And then it wasn't such a machine as this!'

He was standing on the pedals, face crimson with effort. Niall was out of the saddle too, but his legs were whirring round with much more ease and efficiency.

'Change the gears down,' he advised. 'You're going to crack your knees like that!'

'How does one do it?'

'The thumbshifter at your right hand. Put it down to two.'

The man did as instructed and got immediate relief from fighting the high gears. He sat thankfully back onto the saddle as they crested the summit of the road and entered upon what appeared to be a tree-shrouded plateau. Looking ahead of them, in the thin slice of distance visible between the walls of forest that lined the narrow road, they saw the darkening shape of a mountain against the deepening pure blue of the evening sky.

They raced on, fear pumping inexhaustible strength into their aching thighs. They passed and ignored several entrances into the depths of the forest, intent only on putting as much distance as possible between them and their pursuers, pedalling madly on towards the far mountain and the cool slice of sky.

But eventually the man began to slow.

'We should stop somewhere,' he advised himself and Niall. 'We must use the head as well as the legs in this situation.'

Niall was glad enough to let him take command now, and coasted obediently by his side when the man veered off onto a forest track that struck away from the road at a right angle, then after a few hundred yards, turned again somewhat and began to ascend in the direction of the mountain on a path almost parallel to the road below.

They halted at a pile of freshly cut logs and listened for the sound of car engines. But the forest was silent apart from the low buzz of evening insects and the occasional panic-stricken screech of an invisible bird.

'I think we gave them the slip!' said Niall.

'I hope so!' said the man, leaning head down over the handlebars. 'I hope so!'

After a moment, he looked up.

'What is your name, young friend?'

'Niall. Niall Quinn.'

'Well, Niall: I want to give you my most profound gratitude for what you have done for me. Perhaps you have saved my life. I don't know. At the moment, all I can offer you is my hand in humble thanks.'

The man put out his hot hand and Niall took it, enduring the intense grip and the fervent shaking even though he thought it was a bit over the top in the circumstances.

The man let go and climbed off the bike, which he laid against the logs before sitting down wearily. Niall did likewise.

'My name is Jorg Wasserman. It's pronounced Yorg, but if you find that too difficult, you can call me George.'

'You're German,' Niall observed.

The man nodded and wiped the trickling sweat away from his eyes.

'I was just getting into my car to go down to the shopping centre for a bottle of wine when these people grabbed me from behind, tied me and gagged me and blindfolded me, and forced me to lie in the boot of a car. Who they are and what they want I do not know. They said nothing to me, except that they would kill me if I gave them any trouble. I got the impression they are the IRA.'

'No, they're not!' Niall told him. 'They're just ordinary small-time crooks who want to make it look as though you've been kidnapped by the Provos. They think they'll get the ransom money easier that way.'

'How can you know this? You said you are not one of them.'

'Of course I'm not! I overheard them when I was spying on the bike thieves.'

'Bike thieves?' Wasserman was totally confused.

Niall explained very briefly how he had come to be at the farm, and all that he had seen and overheard. When he had finished, Wasserman nodded thoughtfully.

'Well, IRA or not IRA, these men are very dangerous with their guns — especially from what you say about him the one called Gaskin. The sooner we get to the police to tell them, the better.'

'Sure!' Niall agreed. 'But we're out here in the middle of nowhere meantime, and it's going to get dark before too long.'

He shivered and they both looked round. Above them, through the twigs and branches, the blue of the sky was thickening perceptibly, and in the shadows coiled round the gloomy bases of the conifer trunks, night was awake and beginning to spread imperceptibly outwards.

'We are going to be cold soon,' Wasserman agreed. 'And hungry.'

'Listen!' Niall hissed sharply. They both froze into silence as the sound of a motor approached the way they had come along the road below, passed beneath them, and dwindled into the distance.

'Was that them?' Niall whispered urgently, long after the sound had passed.

'Who knows?' said Wasserman. 'If it was, we have been lucky, if it wasn't we have been not so lucky. We have missed a chance of rescue.'

'Come on!' Niall urged as he stood up and remounted his laughably small little bike with its yellow saddle and yellow wheels. 'Let's get a bit further away from the road.'

Wasserman climbed back on his machine and followed him without demur. The rough track rose for a few hundred yards, then doubled back on itself in a sharp hairpin, then another and another. Halfway along each straight section between the sharp bends stood high piles of logs thirty feet or more in length, newly felled and obviously awaiting collection once the next working week began. The logs were laid crosswise on a number of shorter logs, and several stakes were driven into the ground at the front of each pile to prevent it avalanching onto the track.

At the end of another mile of leg-wrenching effort, they dismounted, almost fell off their machines, finally sapped by the all-out effort of their escape bid.

'It is better, I think, that we hide,' Wasserman advised between lung-filling breaths. 'They will never find us in the darkness. We can proceed at dawn.'

Niall looked anxiously back in the direction of the road and his stomach clenched inside him as the sound of the motor returned from the direction in which it had disappeared ten minutes ago, passed under them again, and continued back to its point of origin.

'It *is* them!' he hissed, the pupils of his eyes large and black.

Wasserman nodded with surprising calm. He fumbled in the pocket of his tracksuit top and produced a box of matches and a pipe, which he proceeded to light up.

'They must have realised we took the bikes,' he said between noisy sucks made noisier by the fact that he was still somewhat out of breath. 'They have no doubt searched the main road both ways and satisfied themselves we have not gone that way, now they are desperately hunting these back roads. But they will never find us, I promise you. How many such tracks lead off the road into the forest? Ten? Fifteen? It would take them a week to check every one of them, and they know it. No, they will give up soon and go back to the city to hide themselves. You and me, my young friend Niall, all we have to do is stay out of sight till the morning, and then we are in the clear as you say. Later on, we will light a carefully concealed fire to keep us warm. Then, if only we had something to eat, we would be happy men, eh?'

He grinned, and almost seemed to be enjoying the situation now. Niall gave in to Wasserman's confident predictions of their future and sat down heavily on a log, shoulders sagging with exhaustion. Then he remembered the things Paudge had surrendered to him when he'd started his diet earlier in the day — though it felt to Niall as though that had happened weeks rather than hours ago.

'Hang on,' he said, groping in his pockets. 'I think I might have a few bits and pieces that'll keep us going.'

His jacket fell open, exposing the walkie-talkie on his belt. Wasserman jumped to his feet when he caught sight of it.

'What's that you have?'

'It's a walkie-talkie,' Niall told him. 'I completely forgot about it. My friend Paudge has the other one. I was trying to call him but I think we're out of range.'

'But we must try again!' Wasserman said excitedly. 'Give it to me!'

Niall unclipped the equipment and handed it over. Wasserman seemed familiar with such mysteries and got it going immediately.

'—ty calling. Can you hear me? Over!' said the little loudspeaker abruptly.

Niall leapt to his feet. 'It's Katy! She's calling us!'

'Answer her! Answer her quick!' spluttered Wasserman.

Niall grabbed the walkie-talkie again and pressed the transmit button.

'Hallo, Katy! Hallo, Katy! This is Niall calling you! We can hear you loud and clear! Can you hear this? Over!'

The little loudspeaker hissed tantalisingly for a few seconds before Katy's voice came from it again. But she was repeating the same words as before, and the strength of her transmission was failing rapidly to the point where the final 'over' was scarcely audible.

Niall tried again, desperate.

'Katy! Katy! We're in big trouble. Please answer me. Please!'

Once again, Katy's voice repeated her cool plea for Niall to come in, but this time the strength of the signal rose from almost nothing to being fairly strong.

'What can be happening I wonder?' Wasserman said almost to himself as he sucked grey smoke from the pipe and blew it out in long drifting cones.

Niall continued to plead helplessly for Katy to hear him, and her voice continued robot-like to ask him to do the same in reply, rising and fading away with steady regularity.

'You know,' said Wasserman eventually, 'that almost sounds like she is using a rotating directional antenna. Is that possible?'

Niall glared at the walkie-talkie with a mixture of anger and despair. This time there was only a long hissing silence after his call.

'I give up!' he said and handed the set back to Wasserman.

Wasserman looked at it with pursed lips for a moment and then said, 'Let's just give it one final attempt.'

He cleared his throat. 'Hello, Katy. Hello, Katy. Are you receiving me? Come in please. Come in please, Katy!'

There was a short hiss, then: 'Hello, Niall. This is Katy. If that's you trying to call us back we can't hear you very well. You're very faint. Have you got the booster pack connected? Over.'

'We have! We have! Tell her we have!' Niall was jumping up and down.

'Hello, Katy,' Wasserman answered her. 'We're receiving you very clearly now. The booster is connected. Can you hear us? Over.'

There was no answer, only the hiss again.

Wasserman looked at Niall. 'I think you're right. We must be too far away for her to hear us. But how then can we hear her?'

Niall was too dispirited to care.

'I dunno. Her dad has a mass of ham radio gear up in their attic. Maybe she's using that.'

'Aaah!' said Wasserman, pulling the pipe out of his mouth. 'A radio ham, a funker! So that explains it. In that case, she must have a good aerial and a good receiver, so if we can get a bit higher up . . .'

Katy's voice interrupted him.

'Hello, Niall. This is Katy again. Listen carefully: I can't pick you up on voice transmission. You must be too far away. But there's another way we might be able to do it.'

She then proceeded to give him the instructions on using the morse button, and asked about how he was, was he in danger, and did he have any idea where he was. It was Wasserman who sent the replies.

After Katy told them she and Paudge were going to the guards, and told them to listen out for her every ten minutes, the hiss returned to the little loudspeaker, signalling an outburst of relieved delight by Niall and Wasserman. They linked arms and did a mad little dance in a circle, whooping and yahooing, till the last of their strength left them and they fell back exhausted but grinning onto the logs.

Niall produced a couple of squashed Mars bars and some less recognisable items from his jacket pocket and gave half of them to Wasserman.

'Not exactly health food,' the German quipped cheerily.

'I'd eat anythin' right now,' said Niall. '*Even* health food!'

He and Wasserman took great big bites and chewed gratefully for a few silent moments before Wasserman said:

'We must not rest too long here. We must try to get higher up the mountain. From there, our little walkie-talkie will have a better chance of making itself heard by your friend and by the police. Once they can pinpoint us, we will be, as you say in English, almost out of the woods. Very apt, ja?'

Niall looked up and around. A solitary star twinkled in the rich deep blue above them.

'We'd better hurry, then,' he said, standing up and swallowing the last of his impromptu picnic. 'It's almost dark. We won't be able to see the way much longer.'

'You're right.' Wasserman stood up reluctantly and pulled up his bike. 'But then again, maybe it won't be that dark.'

He pointed above the black tops of the pines. A huge brass-coloured full moon was emerging ponderously into the navy blue sky, attended by one very bright star and drawing the full darkness behind it.

'When I was a youngster in the Pfalz, not quite so young as you,' Wasserman mused while staring at the glowing apparition above them, 'I often went for long treks through the forest by the lights of such a moon. There is a very special kind of feeling, an excitement of a kind, to be so alone among such a silence. Sometimes I used to think I could almost hear the moonlight itself.'

Niall waited, controlling his impatience, while Wasserman stood there entranced by his lunar memories. Sure, it must have been amazing, Mister, Niall thought, but this isn't the time and the place to go dreaming about it.

The dream was abruptly interrupted by the sound of car engines far below them. Niall turned quickly and saw brief flashes of headlights a long way down through the densely packed trunks. He turned back to Wasserman, wide eyes demanding his agreement to run for it.

'Relax, relax,' Wasserman told him almost with amusement. 'They'll never come this way, I told you so already.'

But the sound of the cars came to rest deep down the wooded slopes immediately below them, and died away to inaudibility as they idled. Niall and Wasserman held their breath and waited. The sound of the engines — there seemed to be two — rose again. But instead of continuing off into the distance as before, they remained almost directly below, and more flashes from the headlights began to pierce through the trees.

'They're coming up this track!' Niall burst out almost hysterically.

Wasserman looked both shocked and astonished.

'But how can they know ... Look!'

He pointed down at the track along which they had just come. There, plainly visible in the sharp moonlight, were the two lines cut in the rain-soaked earth by the knobbly tyres of their bicycles.

'Damn!' Niall spat out helplessly.

'They must have checked the entrance to each of the tracks for our trail,' Wasserman concluded grimly. They stood almost hypnotised, watching the distant lights from the car headlamps squirming and twisting their way among the dark shapes of the forest below.

'We'll have to dump the bikes and hide!' said Niall and looked about desperately for the best way to go. 'They're going to catch up with us in a couple of minutes!'

'No!' Wasserman told him sharply. 'I have a better idea. Come and help me.'

They dropped their bikes again and Niall followed Wasserman back to the pile of heavy logs. Wasserman grabbed one of the stakes that held it in place and began working it back and forth to loosen it from the ground.

'Do you understand?' he asked as Niall pulled and pushed from the other side. 'We remove the stakes and the logs will roll on to the path and block it. Then they will have to abandon their cars and follow us on foot if they still want to catch us. But we have the bicycles. Once we are over the top of this hill, we can fly away from them!'

They worked feverishly at the stakes, conscious all the while of the growing drone of the car engines as they wound their way up towards them. Sweat ran into Niall's eyes and made them burn, and splinters of wood slit the skin of his hands, but his mind merely noted the discomfort and the pain and dismissed it. Fear was giving him a mental and physical strength way beyond his years.

The last stake came out and the two jumped back to avoid the expected avalanche of massive trunks. But nothing happened. The pile sat solid and motionless.

'What's holding it? What's wrong?' Niall yelled, almost in tears. Below them, the headlights of the cars were now sweeping aggressively through the massed trunks of the pines as their pursuers negotiated the hairpin bends.

Wasserman suddenly bounded up on top of the logs.

'Get back!' he shouted. 'Get back!'

He heaved and kicked at one of the logs till with a rumble, the whole pile began to fall forward from under him and crash onto the pathway. Niall watched terrified as he leapt from the top of the collapsing heap and disappeared into the darkness under the trees.

'Mr Wasserman! Mr Wasserman!'

The cars were only a few bends away now. Niall snatched up his little bike and mounted, ready to flee on his own.

Wasserman suddenly materialised out of the darkness, unhurt.

'Let's go! They're almost here!' pleaded Niall.

Wasserman jumped astride his machine and together they raced off along the moonlit forest path towards the next hairpin. They were half way up the next straight stretch when the cars scraped round the corner below to confront the jumbled tons of timber blocking their way.

'Halt!' Wasserman ordered Niall in a low voice.

They stopped but stayed astride their machines as the cars a few hundred feet below them pulled up one behind the other in front of the logs. In the brilliant light of the car headlamps, they could see figures emerge to stare at the impenetrable barrier. Angry voices drifted up to them, but mingled with the drone of the engines, the words were unintelligible.

'They will not even be able to turn round on this narrow path!' Wasserman whispered gleefully. 'They will have to reverse all the way down!'

The car engines stopped droning, and the lights of the second one went off.

'They're not going back!' said Niall.

In the dipped beam of the first car, several figures began clambering over the heap of logs.

Wasserman's head dropped forward in dismay. 'What must we do to be rid of these devils?'

'Pedal for your life!' said Niall, and they set off again on their painful struggle upwards.

★　　　★　　　★

'Niall Quinn. Niall Quinn. Niall Quinn ...'

The woman at the hospital reception desk ran her brightly painted fingernail over the list in her book as she muttered the name over and over to herself.

The twins craned their blond heads in through the sliding glass window and tried to spot Niall's entry in the upside-down columns, till the receptionist gave them a frosty look of reproval through her pink-framed spectacles.

'He was brought in this afternoon,' Judith told her as a diversion.

'Fell out of a tree,' said Gwynneth.

'Broke his leg,' Judith added. But the laser gaze continued to burn into them till they wilted back to a respectful distance. Then the woman resumed the search with her elegant finger.

'Niall Quinn,' she eventually announced in a tone indicating the object in question had been located. 'Ward Nine. Turn left at the door, right at the next turning, and it's at the far end of the corridor.'

'Thanks,' the twins muttered and turned to follow her instructions.

'All visitors must be out by eight thirty,' the woman intoned as she reached for a nail file. 'And no smoking!'

The twins stayed close as they negotiated the first corridor, blinking in the harsh glare from the fluorescent lights and the shiny painted walls. The air was thick with a warm hospital smell, intermingled faintly with the aroma of lots of people in their pyjamas.

At the junction of the corridors, they stopped to make way for two white-jacketed porters pushing a trolley with a sleeping woman on it. Then they turned right and scampered along past open ward doors till they reached a plaque that said Ward Nine.

They stood close together at the door and looked around the

beds. There was no sign of Niall. All the patients seemed to be old men, some sitting up in bed, some lying on their sides, others getting out of bed or getting back in again. A nurse was pushing round a metal trolley full of little brown bottles and medical things.

'We're looking for Niall Quinn,' they told her together.

The nurse pointed to a screen that hid a bed in the corner of the ward.

'Mr Quinn? He's over there. He's just had a dressing changed.'

The twins scurried over. Behind the screen, a figure lay buried under the blankets on the bed. They tiptoed up, one on either side of the bed and gently prodded the hidden body where they thought the shoulders should be.

'Niall! Niall!' they said softly.

'It's Judith.'

'And Gwynneth.'

'Are you badly hurt, Niall?'

'Are you in a lot of pain?'

The blankets stirred and sat up. From the midst of them, the head of an ancient little man emerged tortoise-like. His grey hair was nearly all gone, his face was wrinkled and stubbly, and white whiskers protruded from his purply nostrils. But his eyes, despite the puffy lids and the blue bags under them, were as bright as a sparrow's.

'Hello there, girls!' he cackled in a phlegmy voice.

The twins shrank back, dumbfounded.

'Is it me ye've come to see?' he went on, jumping around to get into a more comfortable position. 'Well, well, well! Aren't these hospitals grand places entirely. Clean sheets, three meals a day, and visitors laid on an' all! It's better than a hotel, I'm tellin' ye! If I'd known it was as marvellous as this I'd have come in sooner. This is my first time, ye know. Stuck a garden fork clean through my foot, shoe an' all. Hang on — I'll show ye.'

The twins looked across at each other in horror as he prepared to produce one of his scrawny limbs from the tangle of the bed. They turned in unison to escape, but, quick as a flash, the old man had a grip of both of them by their sleeves.

'Where are ye off to?' he demanded with a gaptoothed grin.

'Visiting time doesn't finish till half eight — ye've half an hour to go!'

They wrenched themselves free and sprinted all the way to the hospital gates.

10

To the Rescue

KATY'S FATHER put the phone down and clenched his lips with an I-thought-as-much look on his face.

'They want us to go down to the garda station,' he announced. 'There's been another big kidnapping by the IRA. All the detectives are flying around checking out suspects.'

'But did they believe you?' Katy insisted.

'The one I spoke to seemed to. Sounded sympathetic enough anyway. But as I said, we'd be foolish just to sit here and wait for them to sort it out when we can do something faster ourselves. Come on!'

His manner had a touch of grimness about it, but at the same time he seemed to be relishing the situation in a boyish kind of a way. He picked up a complex-looking radio receiver he had laid on the hall table while he was phoning the guards. It was a flattish grey box just over a foot square and about three inches thick, with a long, narrow control panel on the front. On top was a rotatable disc marked out in compass points, and from the centre of this protruded a loop of stiff wire about the diameter of a large soup plate.

'Bring the box,' he ordered Paudge, who obeyed promptly by picking up an open plastic shelf tidy full of electrical odds and ends that lay on a chair.

Katy and Paudge followed him towards the front door. As they opened it, the tinkle of laughter and conversation from the kitchen ceased and Katy's mother appeared at the kitchen door. She had a glass of something with a bit of lemon floating in it, and her cheeks were flushed.

'Ah, there you are at last, Liam!' she addressed Katy's father. 'I was just about to start getting the dinner ready this minute. Can you hang on another half an hour or so?'

She smiled a very big smile at him and tipped her head back to look out from under rather bleary eyelids.

'Aaah ... no problem, dear,' he replied, hiding from her gaze behind the rim of his glasses the way Katy did. 'I'm just taking Katy and Paudge with me while I do a quick job. We'll be back shortly. Bye.'

The door shut and the three scurried to Katy's father's car, parked in front of the garage. He put the receiver on the bonnet while he pulled out his keys to open the doors.

'What kind of a yoke is that?' Paudge wondered.

'It's a DF set, direction finding. I bought it years ago when I was thinking of taking up sailing, and never used it. Lucky I never got rid of it, eh? The day after you chuck something out you find you need it, that's always the way.'

The DF set went on the front passenger seat beside Katy's father, and Katy and Paudge tumbled into the back. The car reversed out onto the road with a jolt, turned and sped away.

'What are we going to do?' Paudge asked.

'You tell him, Katy,' said her father, grinning into the rear view mirror. 'I'm sure you've figured it out by now.'

Katy looked at Paudge and smiled. 'Triangulation. We're going to find Niall by triangulation.'

Paudge's forehead wrinkled and gave away his ignorance, but he didn't want to say it out loud, so he merely grunted.

'You see,' she explained kindly, 'we already know what direction from the house Niall was transmitting from. What we do now is drive to a different place, contact him and get him to transmit a signal, and then we can get another bearing on him. When you draw the two lines on a map, the point where they cross each other is where Niall is. Simple.'

Paudge grunted again, then was silent while he digested this.

'But how do we contact him?' he erupted after a minute or so. 'Did you bring the walkie-talkie?'

'No need to,' said Katy's father. 'I've got a portable two-metre outfit in the car. It's handy for having the odd natter when you're on your way from job to job. Wouldn't have the time otherwise.'

He pointed at the parcel shelf under the dashboard and Paudge leaned forward to see the front panel of something very similar to the transceiver up in the attic, only a bit smaller.

'Ah,' he said, and sat back.

The car raced on through the darkening streets where the yellowy orange light from the tall sodium lamps was finally taking over from the daylight. Katy's father hunched forward over the steering wheel, humming something classical-sounding to himself as he drove at crazy speeds through areas Paudge didn't recognise towards the looming blackness of the mountains. Katy slouched far into the corner of the seat, mouth severe, watching the images outside zip past with scarcely blinking eyes.

'Niall'll be all right,' Paudge said almost to himself. 'He can handle himself.'

Katy ignored him and went on watching as the suburbs dissolved away in the rising tide of night and the car bored along through the tunnel carved out by its headlights. Trees leaned over their path, thickly foliaged arms outstretched as if trying to signal them to slow down. From time to time, through the flicker of branches and trunks, she saw the creamy bronze moon, seeming to speed along beside them as it struggled to overcome its own massive inertia and rise to its rightful position above.

Then, suddenly, the road ahead was blocked by a white car and men in dark uniforms with fluorescent orange waistcoats that flared in the headlamps' blaze. A police roadblock checking for the kidnappers.

'Evening, sir,' the garda said when Katy's father had slowed the car to a halt and wound down the window. 'In a hurry?'

'Kind of,' Katy's father nodded uncomfortably.

The policemen wandered round the car, noting its number and shining torches in through the window at the squinting eyes of Katy and Paudge.

'Could I see your licence, please?' the first officer went on. Katy's father rummaged around inside his jacket and produced the red licence.

The guard jotted something in his notebook and then asked, 'Would you mind opening your boot?'

Katy's father hauled himself out and let them gaze in wonder at the tangled mass of electronic indescribables under the boot lid.

'You a TV mechanic or something?' asked one.

'Something like that,' Katy's father agreed.

'What's that on the front seat?'

'Eh ... it's a CB set. We were just going up into the hills to try it out.'

There was a faintly suspicious silence from the policemen, but the first one waved his arm to indicate that they could go.

'Slow down a bit,' he advised, 'you never know what you might run into on these roads.'

Katy's father nodded agreement and blasted off at full throttle.

'Don't you think you should have told them?' Paudge prompted. He didn't think so himself, but he wondered what Katy's father's motives were.

'We'd've been there all night explaining the fine details to them. A fine body of men they may be, but I'm afraid most of them can't cope with a sudden surge of new data, especially if it's unexpected. They just overload and go blank.' He tapped his temple with a finger. 'They just haven't got the hardware up here.'

Paudge smiled secretly in the darkness of the rear seat. It always pleased him to hear adults say out loud the things he thought to himself.

They roared on for many more miles before stopping in a disused little layby at the side of a road that corkscrewed its way carefully upwards into the moonlit hills.

'We'll try here,' Katy's father announced with open enthusiasm. He jumped out and put the DF set on the roof of the car, and then began connecting up wires from the back of it to the underside of the transceiver hooked onto the parcel shelf. Katy and Paudge got out to watch as he grunted and muttered to himself, lying on the passenger seat to screw connections tight, then finally producing an antenna with a magnetic base which he plonked on the roof with a thud.

'There!' he said, once he had the final cable in place. 'All ready to fire up. Just have to sit it on the walkie-talkie frequency.'

He switched on the transceiver in the car, unclipped the little microphone that was hanging beside it, and held it out to Katy.

'D'you want to do the honours?'

She took the microphone and climbed into the passenger seat.

'Hello, Niall. Hello, Niall. This is Katy calling you again. Are you receiving me? Over.'

Once again, an unbroken hiss came from the loudspeaker in the dashboard. She tried twice, three times, five times, but there was no answer from out there among the round peaks and hidden valleys. Paudge and Katy's father looked out across the ash-coloured landscape broken here and there by the black huddles of forest, as if they expected to see Niall waving to them in the distance.

'I told him to keep listening for us!' Katy said eventually in annoyance.

'He said yes when you asked him if he was in danger,' Paudge reminded her. 'Maybe he's being chased. Maybe they've caught him.'

Katy's father looked across the ashen landscape again and considered the situation, his expression showing a determination not to be daunted.

'Maybe we're in the wrong place. Maybe he's on the other side of those hills. Gimme that map.'

Katy handed him the map on which they had drawn a line showing the direction of Niall's weak signals. He held 't in the bright glare of the car headlights, tracing the contours with a finger.

'Right!' he announced crisply, folding up the map and handing it back to Katy. 'Let's get a move on!'

'Where are we going?' Paudge asked.

Katy's father put the DF set and the antenna back in the car.

'Over the hills and far away. Well, not so far really. The highest point in the road's about eight or nine miles over there.' He waved an arm at the dull-gleaming silence of the hills. 'We'll have the best chance from there.'

'But we could spend the whole night doing this!' Katy protested.

'Don't worry, we'll find him, I know we will.'

'How can you know that?' Paudge said with low-browed scepticism.

Katy's father took in a deep breath and let it out again, slowly. 'Well, you see, Paudge, intelligence and reasoning are a bit like the stages on a rocket launcher — they blast you out of whatever's holding you back. But when you're getting close to the right orbit, you ditch them and make minor course corrections with spurts from a good old-fashioned hunch. Right now, my hunch tells me we're not far off target. Jump in and let's go.'

Oh, very clever, thought Paudge, but I still don't believe it.

He and Katy climbed back in and slammed the doors, and the car growled away up the metallic spiral of the road.

11

Closing In

GASKIN TRAMPED INTENTLY up the forest track, jabbing the bulk of PJ in the small of the back with the snout of his gun every now and then to force the pace. The light from the torch in his unarmed hand wavered along the thin tracks made by the bicycle tyres in the brown gravelly earth, while the other members of his gang, coming behind, poked the beams of their handlamps in under the surrounding walls of sleeping trees, just in case.

PJ trudged along at his own lumbering speed, ignoring the goading from behind except for a rhythmic contraction of the muscles under his ears. The full moon was now high in the star-spattered night sky, and its cold light conjured a world of stark black-and-white contrast around them. On PJ's face, it painted a strange stony expression, like that on a statue of an eyeless Greek god, gazing at a fixed point miles away inside his head.

'You'll never catch them,' he said in a flat monotone, without turning.

'Shurrup!' Gaskin spat back. He gave PJ another jab in the back without lifting his eyes from the bicycle tracks.

'He might be right,' one of the men behind ventured after a silence broken by the soft trudge of their feet. 'They're on bikes remember.'

'They'll burn themselves out soon,' Gaskin snarled. 'They can't keep this up much longer. They've been goin' for hours now. They'll have to get off an' walk soon, an' then we've got them!'

'They only have to get to the top of the hill, an' then it's downhill all the way for them,' PJ told him.

'Shurrup!' Gaskin ordered even more viciously, and hit him on the shoulder blade with the butt of the gun. PJ trudged on without flinching.

'I'm sure lookin' forward to findin' out who the second one is,' said another of Gaskin's entourage.

'One a' PJ's boys, isn't it? Somebody he conveniently forgot to tell us about!' Gaskin's voice rose as he again tried to make some physical impression on PJ from behind.

'I told you already,' PJ replied with explosive calmness, 'I don't know who he is. There's only the three of us at the farm. I'm just as baffled about it as anybody.'

'Oh, sure!' mocked Gaskin. 'Somebody just happened to be passin' by, out there, at the backend of nowhere! Very convenient, eh?'

He took his eyes momentarily off the tracks and raised the gun to vent his fury again on the dark expanse of PJ's back. But before the gleaming weapon could fall, one of the men interrupted.

'Gaskin! Look!'

The torch beams congregated on one spot on the ground. Beside the bicycle tyre marks, two sets of footprints suddenly appeared.

'See? I told you!' Gaskin said with delight, his teeth hardly parting for the words. 'They're pushing now — we've got'm!'

With a startling explosion of physical power, PJ leapt off the

105

moonlit path and was swallowed up in the darkness of the downhill slope. Gaskin and the others stood in startled immobility for a few seconds while the noise of PJ's bulky frame crashing through branches and over fallen rotting timber receded steadily downwards and away. Then the men turned quickly to Gaskin, mutely awaiting his orders.

Gaskin raised his gun with both hands and began firing regular shots in the direction of the noise. He fired four times, each report echoing with painful loudness through the shrouded forest. When the last one died away, they listened to the moonlit silence.

'D'ya think ya hit'm?' one of the men asked in a low voice that betrayed a definite lack of enthusiasm at the idea.

'I hope it blew his head off!' The words had great difficulty wriggling free from Gaskin's clenched jaw.

'Ssshhh! Listen!' hissed another man.

From behind them, in the upward direction of the path, came sounds of movement, and a noise that sounded like a stifled cry of fear.

Gaskin jumped round, PJ's fate forgotten in the instant.

'It's them!' he hissed urgently. 'C'mon — run!'

They galloped off round the next bend in the path, panting and gradually slowing as the unaccustomed exertion got the better of them. After a few hundred yards, Gaskin held up his gun and they halted to listen again. Something was stirring cautiously in the invisibility above the road. Gaskin gave silent orders to the men to spread out.

'Come out with yer hands up!' he yelled in his high-pitched voice.

Nothing happened for several seconds. Then the darkness into which they were staring tensely suddenly erupted and a torrent of fantastically horned shapes charged at them, swept past on either side, and disappeared the way PJ had gone.

Gaskin and his henchmen were momentarily terrified till they realised what it was — a herd of deer. Then one of the gang swung round and began firing his weapon madly after them.

'Madman!' yelled Gaskin, knocking the weapon to the ground. 'What the hell are ya doin' that for?'

The man looked resentfully abashed at his loss of control.

'The brother's a butcher,' he explained awkwardly. 'We go huntin' sometimes. They're worth a good bit ...'

Gaskin gave him a shove.

'Get movin' — it's two-legged meat we're after!'

*   *   *

Niall and Wasserman halted abruptly when they heard the first volley of shots crackling through the trees and echoing angrily around them.

'What's that?' said Niall, with a new note of fear in his voice.

'They're shooting,' Wasserman answered. 'But at what? And why?'

They waited in the deep shadow at the side of the path and listened. Not even a sigh of wind moved among the trees.

'Come!' Wasserman ordered after quite a few seconds had passed. 'We must keep moving!'

He leaned on the handlebars of his bicycle to force it up the increasingly steep slope, but stopped when he realised Niall wasn't following.

'I can't!' Niall explained, and his voice was thick and shaky. 'My legs! My legs are too weak! They won't ...'

'But you must!' Wasserman insisted. 'They are coming, with guns!'

Niall leaned over the saddle of his machine and let out a sound close to a sob. Wasserman watched him for a moment, then looked around with a desperate lunar glint in his eyes.

'Come this way!' he hissed at Niall, and steered his bike off the path into a gap between the towering trunks. 'We will try to fool them by going through the trees. They will see our tracks have left the path, but perhaps we can hide from them. Quickly now!'

Niall obeyed mechanically. It was almost totally dark under the trees, and the ground was rough and strewn with brittle broken branches, but Wasserman was somehow able to force his way ahead and Niall, close behind him, found it easier to go across the slope than to go up it.

A hundred yards or so into the canopy of invisibility, they abruptly emerged onto a small clearing drenched in still moonlight. Stumps of tree trunks jutted up through piles of freshly dead branches, and at the downslope end of the clearing several newly felled trees sprawled across each other like enormous corpses.

The second volley of shots split the silence again, but this time more muffled.

'Over there!' hissed Wasserman. He pointed diagonally up the clearing to where the moonlight cut a slender gap between the motionless pines.

Niall struggled along behind him, fighting a growing sick feeling in his stomach and shivering as the sweat trapped against his skin cooled in the night air of the forest. Once out of the clearing, there was no more debris clawing at their legs and wheels, and they found themselves on a narrow but clearly lit path that climbed gently across the slope.

'Just a little more,' Wasserman pleaded, looking anxiously at Niall. 'Then we can rest.'

Niall nodded silently and bent his head back to the exhausting task of pushing on and up. He became sharply aware of the trudging motion of his legs as he toiled along behind Wasserman, but with a curious detachment, as if he was an independent observer merely noting the passing of painful seconds and minutes.

He had no idea how long they had staggered along the path like this when Wasserman came to a halt ahead of him.

'Please!' Niall panted. 'Stop. I can't do it any more!'

'I don't think you have to. Look.'

Wasserman swept his arm theatrically across the vista of ghostly landscape that had arisen before and below them. They had emerged from the trees onto the bare shoulder of the mountain, and were standing on a wide track recently churned up by heavy machinery. To their right, it led back into the black forest that clothed the head of the mountain, and to their left, it wound downwards over a wide bare moonlit expanse dotted with tree stumps and massive boulders jutting from the earth. Here and there, a skeletal dead tree stripped of bark and branches gleamed in the icy light.

'We have made it,' he announced quietly, more with relief than elation. 'From here on it is downhill to safety.'

Niall looked down the muddy road, then closed his eyes.

'I've got to rest for a bit. I've got to.'

Wasserman looked around.

'Over there,' he said, indicating a stack of boulders flanked by heaps of lopped branches on the other side of the road.

Niall followed him across. Wasserman kicked his way through the brittle twigs so they could get round to the back of the boulders. There they found a sheet of rusty corrugated steel thrown across between two low rocks to form a crude shelter. In front of it was a black patch surrounded by small stones where someone had lit a fire.

'The foresters must have used this,' he guessed. 'Wait.'

He tore out some of the tall fern heads that were growing around the boulders and heaped them under the shelter.

'Lie down there,' he told Niall. 'We will rest for ten minutes, no more. Okay?'

'Okay.' Niall collapsed gratefully onto the ferns.

Wasserman looked around anxiously, gnawing his lower lip as he tried to work out their next move. When he glanced down at Niall's huddled shadow after a few moments, the slow sound of deep breathing told him the boy had slipped into an exhausted sleep. Wasserman unzipped the jacket of his tracksuit and crouched down to spread it over Niall's shoulders. As he did so his hand bumped against something hard under Niall's jacket. It was the walkie-talkie.

'Of course!' Wasserman muttered to himself triumphantly, even forgetting to switch back to his native tongue. 'We forgot about that in our excitement!'

He picked it up. The booster pack was disconnected and missing, probably still clipped to Niall's unconscious body, but he switched it on anyway in the hope that he might be able to hear something without having to disturb the exhausted boy.

The loudspeaker hissed emptily for a second or two — then he was startled as Katy's voice, loud and exasperated in tone, barked into the still night.

'Hello, Niall! Hello, Niall! Can you hear me! Come in *please*!'

Wasserman nearly dropped the walkie-talkie in his excitement. He pressed down the transmit switch.

'Hello, Katy! Hello, Katy! We can hear you loud and clear! Can you hear this?'

There was a short hissing silence, then:

'Whoever's on this frequency will you please get off immediately! This is an emergency!'

'Hello, Katy!' Wasserman spluttered back, 'You don't understand. My name is Wasserman, I was kidnapped and Niall helped me escape. He is here beside me, sleeping. Can you hear this? Over!'

There was another hissing silence, longer this time, then Katy's father's voice replied.

'Hello, Wasserman. We hear you quite clearly. Are you all right? Is Niall all right?'

'Yes, yes, we are okay, just exhausted. The kidnappers are chasing us through the forest. Niall can't go on any more, so we are hiding from them. Can you get the police to us? Hurry!'

'We're just getting a fix on your exact position right now. I don't suppose you've any idea where you are, over?'

Wasserman looked down the moonlit bare slope and across a wide flat wilderness to where another roundshouldered mountain cloaked in dark trees rose against the glinting stars. Low down and far away some shreds of cloud glowed faintly orange. Perhaps that was some reflection of the city's lights, he thought.

'No, no idea.'

'Well, here's what we want you to do. At the side of the walkie-talkie, you'll find a little slide switch. When you push that down, the unit transmits a continuous signal. Turn that on and put it in the open somewhere near you. Between ourselves and the guards, we'll be able to track you down in no time. Got that?'

'Yes,' Wasserman confirmed when he found the slide switch.

'Good,' said Katy's father. 'Now do what I said, and don't move too far away unless you absolutely have to. We'll be with you in person soon.'

Wasserman replied with one word, 'Hurry!', before he pushed

the slide switch and the loudspeaker went dead. He looked around for somewhere to put the unit as instructed, and his eye ran up to the top of the pile of boulders. He scrambled up them, sat the walkie-talkie on the highest point, and listened for any sound of their pursuers coming up through the forest before he climbed carefully down to the shelter.

Wasserman checked the time on his watch by its nightlight, then looked down at the unconscious Niall with a frown. After a moment, his eyes turned to the bikes, half-gleaming and half-invisible in the moonlight. His eyebrows moved up and down as he thought, then his expression changed suddenly.

'It's worth a try,' he muttered, again in English. 'For sure it is!'

He picked up the bikes one by one and wheeled them back to the muddy road. Then he returned and knelt beside Niall in the little shelter, tucking the tracksuit jacket carefully round the boy's sides.

'Farewell, my young friend,' he whispered. 'Till we meet again.'

He stood up and began making his way back to the road, moving backwards and filling in the path they had made through the debris and ferns by pulling branches and loose vegetation into it as he went. Once at the road, he wheeled the bikes across to where they had emerged from the forest, and listened. Below, muffled by the dark mass of trees, he could hear the echoing sounds of the pursuers advancing slowly but steadily upwards, snarling briefly at each other from time to time.

Hurriedly, Wasserman took a dead branch and scrubbed all trace of his and Niall's footsteps from the mud on the road, so that there was no sign of their ever having made their way into the tangle of fern and debris that hid the shelter and Niall. This done, Wasserman threw his leg over his bike while holding onto Niall's, and set off down the rutted road with both machines, wobbling precariously as he descended into the darkness waiting below.

12

Trickery

THE POLICEMEN manning the roadblock scattered nervously to the sides of the road when Katy's father slid the car to a halt behind them.

'We found them! We've got them pinpointed!' he shouted, jumping out and running towards them.

'Found who?' a sergeant demanded with a certain amount of hostility. He and the other guards came cautiously forward, shielding their eyes from the still glaring headlights and ready for action.

Katy and Paudge stayed in the back of the car while Katy's father told their story and instructed the silent officers as to what they should do next. The two youngsters were worn out by events and by so much unaccustomed late-night activity and were happy now to leave it all in the hands of adults, for better or worse.

'He has to be all right, he has to!' Katy assured herself quietly.

Paudge felt a little pinch of irritation inside. Fatigue was making him cranky.

'All this would never have happened if he hadn't got himself that fancy racing bike,' he complained. 'He should have stuck to a BMX like I told him.'

'Why shouldn't he have a racing bike if he wants one?' Katy retorted. 'I'm sure he was getting fed up with BMX — you can't go on doing the same things all the time.'

'Why not!' It was more an assertion than a question.

'Because ... 'cos people change, that's why. They grow up.'

Paudge snorted and skulked deeper into the seat.

'Who wants to grow up?'

Katy looked at his surly tired features in the shadows. She remembered the summers when they were seven and eight, when she and Niall and Paudge had such great times roaming the wild corners around their area, playing in the streets and in each other's homes. She and Paudge had a makeshift train made from her tricycle with the back part of another one lashed on behind, and they had spent so many exhilarating hours on it whizzing down the streets and terrifying the younger kids. They really did have great times then.

But that was before the crash that killed Paudge's father.

'I suppose we all have to grow up whether we want to or not,' she said eventually. And as she said it, she realised without being able to put it into words that this was Paudge's problem: he just didn't want to grow up. He wanted nothing to change, everything to stay all fun and sunshine like it was back then when they were younger and his father was still alive.

'I don't see adults having much fun out of life,' Paudge growled. 'Always moaning about money and weighed down by worries about one thing or another. It hasn't got much to recommend it.'

A wash of sympathy for him swept through Katy. The whole neighbourhood knew his mother had had a terrible struggle to fend for the two of them on her own, and poor Paudge must have shared in her sufferings too. Maybe he even felt a bit guilty because of it.

Katy felt an impulse to touch him to show what she felt, that she understood. But before she could do anything about it, her father stuck his head in and beamed an announcement at them.

'They've just been on the radio to their superiors. They're sending up a couple of army jeeps with proper tracking equipment, so it'll all be over in an hour or so.'

'Great,' mumbled Paudge, and curled up with a tired sigh. 'Wake me up when it happens.'

★   ★   ★

Gaskin emerged from the dark of the forest and stood looking down at the churned-up mud road while his henchmen stumbled up to join him one at a time. They breathed heavily through open mouths leaving little puffs of steam hanging in the sharp moonlit air, and their shoulders heaved as they recovered from the battle with the wild mountain slope.

'They must be half way to the nearest garda station by now!' the man next to him spat. 'They're on a downhill run now. I'm gettin' outa here before it's too late!'

But he and the others stood frozen in the moonlight, waiting to see what Gaskin would do.

Gaskin said nothing. He took in a long slow breath and let it out again with a wet snort. His cheeks sank in as he gripped the insides of his mouth between his molars.

'What now, Gaskin?' asked another man. 'Back to the cars?'

Gaskin still said nothing. He shone the beam of his torch onto the mud at their feet. The ruts cut by Wasserman with the two bikes only minutes earlier were sharp and unmistakable in the gooey earth.

Gaskin swung the torch beam round. It crossed the gap which Wasserman had closed with branches, but he noticed nothing. It swept across the stack of boulders behind which Niall was hidden and asleep, and back onto the muddy path as it led upwards and into the forest again. Then he swung it quickly round again and turned to the men.

'Just a mo,' said the one beside him. 'What was that?'

He shone his own torch on the boulders, probing up and around till the beam came to rest on the walkie-talkie unit sitting on top of the stack, its little antenna glinting in the light.

'Go see,' Gaskin ordered tersely.

The man struggled up the rocks, slipping once or twice, then slithered down again.

'It's some kind of a walkie-talkie,' he said as he examined it by torchlight. 'How'd it get up there?'

Gaskin grabbed it from him and squinted at it. He pressed some of the controls, but nothing happened.

'It's a dud. Throw it away.'

'Give it here!' demanded the one who had shot at the deer herd. 'It might be worth a few bob.'

Gaskin threw it at him contemptuously, and the man caught it and pushed the antenna down as far as it would go before shoving the unit in one of the deep pockets of his anorak. None of them had noticed the continuous transmission switch at the side.

'Let's go, Gaskin,' said the man at his side. 'We blew it, might as well admit it. We're only askin' for more trouble, hangin' about like this.'

Gaskin said nothing, but continued looking down the track for a few moments while his brain tried to make the connections between suspicion and evidence. Then, abruptly, he turned through the group of waiting men and went galloping back the way they had come.

'Move it! Fast!'

The henchmen followed smartly, the one with the walkie-talkie in his pocket bringing up the rear.

*   *   *

The banging of car doors startled Paudge out of his uncomfortable slumbers.

He sat up, trying to uncrumple his face and force his sticky eyelids to obey the command to open. It wasn't quite so dark outside the car, and in the grainy gloom he could make out Katy and her dad talking to two guards and a soldier. Further along the road, an army vehicle with several different shapes of antenna on top was parked at an angle on the verge.

Paudge winced in agony when a leg that had gone to sleep began to wake up too with a surge of fierce pins and needles. The group outside split up and Katy and her father walked back to the car while the others faded into the predawn shadows.

'What's happening?' Paudge croaked to Katy when she climbed in beside him. His voice was only half-awake too.

Katy and her father looked less enthusiastic now and more serious.

'Nobody knows,' she said. 'They lost the signal for a while, then they picked it up again. But it's very weak — we'd never have been able to pick it up ourselves — and it seems to be moving all the time.'

Paudge stretched his prickling leg and rubbed, almost punched, his eyes.

'They must be on the run again!'

Katy nodded without looking at him. The car started up and moved, following the army jeep and the police cars in front of it at a distance.

'At least we must be closing in on them fast,' Paudge added hopefully.

'So are the kidnappers by the looks of things,' Katy's father said over his shoulder.

'We must get to them first!' said Katy.

'Well, even if we don't we'll still be able to home in on them. But if the kidnappers are there too, it's obviously going to mean problems.'

'They'll be armed?' Paudge said questioningly.

'Undoubtedly.'

They drove on slowly as the tight convoy picked its way through the dissolving darkness.

'At least,' said Katy's father, 'we won't have to wait much longer to find out what's going to happen.'

★   ★   ★

Niall also felt very uncomfortable when he awoke. His clothes were wet and he was shivering with cold. For a moment, he had no idea where he was, and the unaccustomed feel of the damp ferns against his face startled him so much that he sat up suddenly and banged his head on the low metal roof of the makeshift shelter.

He slumped down again, clutching his head as the shock sliced through it like ice, his face scrunched up against the pain. He lay still for a long time till the feeling passed away and normal brain function gradually returned. Slowly, he began to figure out where he was and how he had come to be here. The events of the night before flickered through his memory like fast snatches of film till they arrived at the moment when he fell asleep and everything, even the fear, had gone blank.

But looking out from under the shelter, there was something very different about the world now, something that made it feel a far less hostile place than it had been when he crawled into his hiding place. His still-tired mind had to struggle for several

116

moments before arriving at the obvious but astonishing explanation: light.

'It's getting light!' he mumbled in amazement as if it was something he had never expected to see again. 'It's the dawn!'

He sat up again, warily keeping his head low, and crawled out stiffly and carefully into the small clearing in front of the shelter. The crushed grass was sodden with dew which soaked into his already saturated clothes, making them cling to his skin as he staggered to his feet. The sky above was now a rich morning blue and all but the brightest stars had dissolved in the growing brightness. The moon was still there, but faded and distant and much smaller looking. Behind the dark trees in what was evidently the east, ribs of high cloud like the wave marks on a beach were soaking up the advance offerings of stunning colours from the still hidden sun.

Niall stood staring at the slow explosion of the new day till another difference in his circumstances hit him: Wasserman was gone!

He spun round several times, eyes searching everywhere desperately, but he couldn't even see the path out of the clearing. He inflated his lungs to let out a shout, but the suddenly remembered terror of his pursuers stopped it in his throat.

Then he heard a sound. Something was moving out there among the ferns and branches. Coming towards him. He turned and ran blindly, not choosing any particular direction, crashing through the dense wet vegetation in silent panic until suddenly he ran into something. *Someone!*

'Hold on, there, take it easy! It's only me, your old friend!'

Niall looked into Wasserman's face, and then threw his arms round him in a hug of sheer relief.

'I thought it was them! I thought ...'

'I know, I know,' Wasserman told him reassuringly. 'But it's all right now. They've gone. We're safe.'

'Gone? How can you be sure ...?'

'Because I tricked them. I made them give up.'

Niall frowned a silent question.

'I hid the way into this place, and then rode down the road on both bikes so they would see the tracks and think we both escaped down the mountainside too fast for them to follow. And it worked. At least I think it did. I stopped about a kilometre down and waited but they did not come. Of course, maybe they turned back before they reached the road, I don't know. Anyway, they are not here anymore, the forest is silent and deserted. Apart from us. All we have to do now is find our way back to civilisation.'

Niall shuddered and sagged and Wasserman stopped him from falling.

'Exhausted? So am I. We must find some place soon to get out of these damp clothes or we will suffer exposure. Do you think you can still cycle? It will warm us up a bit.'

Niall nodded, clutching his arms around himself against the dewy cold.

'Also the sun will rise soon and its rays will heat us,' Wasserman added. They both looked to the opposite horizon from the setting moon, where more flimsy cloud, stretched out thin against the startling pale blue of space, was flaring with the hot colours that announce a summer dawn.

'How can it be coming up again?' Niall wondered. 'It's hardly any time since it set.'

'Night is very short at this time of year ..'

Wasserman's voice trailed off as he noticed the top of the boulders.

'The walkie-talkie!'

He scrambled up to the top of the rocks and stood there looking round. Then he bounded down, jubilation on his face.

'They have been here! There are footprints on the road and mud marks on the rocks. They must have seen the walkie-talkie and taken it. But they did not find our little hiding place here — they must have assumed we escaped down the road! We're safe!'

He shook Niall by the shoulders and gave him a quick hug. But Niall was less overjoyed.

'If we don't have the walkie-talkie, how can we get in touch with Katy again? How will they know where we are?'

'Ah!' said Wasserman, suddenly serious again. 'While you were asleep I had a conversation with your Katy and her father. They were much nearer us, here in the mountains in a car. The man told me how to leave the radio on so that they could track the continuous signal. They were going to get police help. That's why I put the walkie-talkie up there, to give the signal a better chance.'

'D'you think they had time to track this position?'

Wasserman shrugged. 'We can't be sure.'

'What do we do then? Stay here and wait for them to find us, or go looking for help?'

Wasserman pulled the pipe and matches from his pocket while he thought. He struck a match and was just about to put it into the pipe bowl when he stopped and stared at the flame.

'Aha. Now, why did I not think of that before?'

He put the pipe back in his pocket and began gathering up bits of broken branches and twigs.

'We'll light a fire to dry our clothes and warm ourselves, and if there's no sign of rescuers when we've done that, we can set off on the bicycles again. Agreed?'

Niall nodded. The prospect of being warm and dry appealed to him above all other considerations right now, and he too began to gather up fuel for the promised fire.

★   ★   ★

'Gaskin, this is askin' for trouble! The longer we hang about this area with that German on the loose and half the guards in the country out lookin' for him, the bigger the risk. We should head back to town and disappear!'

The driver threw the car round the bends of the boreen to show his anger, but Gaskin kept staring straight ahead as he swung from side to side, his expression malevolently impassive.

'We will,' he assured the man tersely, 'we will. But first we've got to put our friend PJ and his fellow clowns out of business for a while.'

The driver glanced sideways at him.

'Whadya mean?'

'I mean I'm gonna burn the place an' everythin' in it.'

The driver let a snort of impatience and incredulity.

'What good's that gonna do us?'

'It's gonna make me feel a bit better. It's gonna let him know the kind of thing that's in store for him when I do catch up with him. And I will.'

'You still think it was one of them that split with the German?'

'Who else could it've been?'

The car scraped to a halt in the farmyard again before the driver had time to offer an opinion. Gaskin got out immediately and went into the house, hard-faced and silent. When the driver stepped out of the car, he heard the muffled cries of the imprisoned Doyler and O'Brien coming from the bicycle shed, and he jogged quickly over and went in.

'You two'd better get outa this place pretty smart!' he advised them, and quickly undid the knots that bound them together. 'Gaskin's gone ape. He's gonna burn this place an' he wouldn't care if you were still inside it or not, I've seen that look on his face before!'

Doyler and O'Brien did not wait to be told twice. Without uttering a word, they scuttled out of the shed like startled rats and fled over the wall into the dawn-bright wilderness beyond.

The second car had arrived and the other men were standing in front of the farmhouse watching smoke pouring through windows that had been broken from inside.

'What's he up to now?' one of them demanded.

'Burnin' the place.'

'What for?'

'You know Gaskin,' the driver shrugged.

Flames rose behind the little windows of the cottage. The front door opened and a billowing pall of black smoke fell out, with Gaskin at its centre, not even coughing. He marched across to the bicycle shed, ignoring the men gathered round the cars, and went in.

'Ah come on!' said the man with the walkie-talkie in his pocket. 'Let's get goin' an' leave him to it! He's behavin' like a schoolgirl now!'

The men from the second car all got back in again, and it executed a reverse turn in preparation for heading back down the boreen.

'You comin' or are ya stayin' with the madman?' demanded the man with the walkie-talkie, leaning out of a rear window.

The driver looked at him and then at the shed.

'You go on ahead,' he said.

The car roared away down the dirty boreen.

Gaskin reappeared from the shed, leaving the door open for air to feed the snarling flames that were already licking round the rows of smartly-painted bicycles inside.

'Are ya finished yet, are ya?' the driver asked aggressively.

Gaskin ignored him, took out his gun, and fired several loudly reverberating shots into the side of the already disabled van where the fuel tank was. There was a ripping explosion that sent them both staggering backwards and the van erupted with searing fire. They both stood looking at it for a few moments, then Gaskin turned to survey the growing infernos that were savagely devouring the ancient timbers of the house and the shed.

'Does it make ya feel any better?' asked the driver.

'It would if PJ was inside,' Gaskin replied quietly. 'Let's move!'

They got into the car, reversed it and shot off down the boreen at speed.

★   ★   ★

Katy's father braked his car to a halt as the convoy in front stopped and one of the guards came running back towards them.

'You can't come any further!' the officer told them. 'The army boys picked up the signal again very strong, and so did the other group, so they got a good fix on them. They're up there somewhere.'

He waved his arm towards the side of the road where the horizontal rose-gold light of the rising sun showed them the grey boreen walls twisting away towards the invisible farm.

'Why can't we go with you to meet them?' Katy demanded indignantly.

'There's a good chance the kidnappers are in the vicinity too,' her father told her. 'We'd get in the way if there was any trouble.'

'Exactly,' said the officer. 'Our lads are going in on foot from here, just in case.'

121

Another army truck and more garda cars approached along the main road from the other direction and halted at the boreen entrance. There were about a dozen uniformed men now, some of them obviously very senior by the look of them, and about as many others in ordinary clothes. These men carried a variety of guns and personal radios, and after quick discussions with the senior officers, set off up the boreen at a smart trot.

'Maybe we shouldn't even be this close!' said Paudge apprehensively as they watched the men go.

From far in the distance came the faint sound of Gaskin's gun. Everybody — soldiers, policemen, Paudge, Katy and her father — froze for a brief second before turning to look in the direction from which the sound had begun its journey. There, rising from the folds of the bleak landscape, were the first plumes of smoke from the blazing farm buildings.

'What's going on?' Katy said as she and Paudge and her father all scrambled out of the car for a better view.

'Stay here and don't move any closer!' the officer warned them before he ran back to the others.

'Why are they shooting?' It was a plea for reassurance from Paudge rather than a question. Katy's father quietly put his arms round both their shoulders. Some birds were chirruping madly on the telephone wires above them as the new day warmed their feathers.

'Let's just wait and see,' he advised.

It was all over fairly quickly. First they heard the sound of the kidnap gang's car coming helter-skelter down the boreen. There were several sharp cracks of gunfire — warning shots from the armed detectives on the boreen — and the car halted. A minute or two later, it appeared at the boreen entrance driven by a police officer. Two of the gang were in the back with other detectives crushed in beside them, and the other two kidnappers, one of them still with the walkie-talkie in his pocket, followed on foot, dragged along at a fast trot by the officers they were handcuffed to.

'They got them! They got them!' Paudge burst out, jumping up and down and clapping his hands in delight.

Then came the sound of the second car with Gaskin in it. Again there was the sharp rattle of automatic gunfire in warning and the car slowed to a noisy halt. There was one loud shot in reply, but no more. Then the second car appeared on the road driven by a detective, with Gaskin and his driver held firmly in the back by his triumphant captors.

'Now where is Niall and the man they kidnapped?' wondered Katy's father. The three of them started towards the milling crowd of policemen and soldiers round the gang and their cars, but the officer who had spoken to them came jogging back.

'Where are they?' Katy demanded.

'The gang say Wasserman, the German, escaped into the forest, but they claim they don't know anything about your friend, Niall.'

'But how did the army guys track the walkie-talkie signal here?' protested Paudge.

'One of the mob had it in his pocket,' the policeman explained. 'Says he found it in the forest. Maybe your friend dropped it in the heat of the chase. Anyway, it was still switched on, that's why we kept picking up the signal.'

The other three looked at each other in anxious perplexity.

'Do you believe them?' Katy's father asked the officer.

The policeman looked as perplexed as they were.

'It's a strange business right enough,' he agreed. 'But we'll probably sort it out soon enough now we've got the villains safely apprehended. That fire's in a farm they said was used by some bunch of bicycle thieves, so once the boys get up there they might find something that'll straighten it all out for everybody.'

'Could Niall be up there in that fire?' said Paudge.

The officer shook his head.

'The villains were quite definite about that, and I believe them.'

Three police cars sped past them taking Gaskin and his gang away to the city and their prison cells. Katy's eyes came in contact with Gaskin's cold gaze for a microsecond as they flashed past, and even though she had not seen his face in the shadows of the car's interior, she shivered involuntarily.

'Well, at least he's not in danger from those horrors any more!'

The policeman nodded agreement.

'They said there's another couple of characters on the loose out there somewhere, but they're not part of that mob, they're only small-timers running to save their skins. We'll herd them in as the day wears on, once we get a proper search of the forest organised for your fellah and the German.'

Katy and her father and Paudge all shifted their gaze to the thick green walls of the forest that rose upwards to the distant round peaks.

'Poor Niall,' said Katy, her bleary eyes watery with tiredness and emotional strain. 'After all this, lost in the forest!'

13

Breakfast

BUT TO NIALL and Wasserman, things no longer seemed that bad.

They had built a blazing fire in front of the little shelter, stripped off to their underwear and hung the damp clothing on sticks pushed into the ground near the heat of the flames, then sat down to bask themselves in the fire's reviving glow.

The sun rose slowly and began adding its contribution to their growing feeling of well-being by massaging their backs gently with its strengthening rays. Niall found one last crushed and deformed Mars bar in his jacket pocket, and they breakfasted on this, sipping drops of dew from the broad ferns afterwards.

Wasserman lit his pipe and puffed the last shreds of tobacco in its bowl, looking incongruously relaxed and contented as he stared at the flames.

'And you say they are not the IRA, these kidnappers?' he suddenly inquired.

Niall nodded. The heat from the fire was magnifying his tiredness.

'I overheard them at the farm. They wanted you and the guards to believe they were. They thought they'd get the ransom easier.'

Wasserman put his head back and laughed with his eyes closed.

'If only they knew? My company would not pay one penny to get me back, not one!'

'Why not?'

'Because they want to get rid of me. I was making too much of a nuisance of myself in Stuttgart, criticising too much, suggesting too many new ideas. My chief, he does not like this. So I am sent to manage the Irish branch, because they know it is doing badly and very soon they will have to close it, and then they have the chance to get rid of me. You understand?'

'Doesn't sound very nice of them.'

'That's the way it is in the working world, I'm afraid. Remember that, my young friend, when the time comes for you to go out into it.'

'If you know they want to get rid of you, why do you stay with them?'

Wasserman took a long draw at his pipe and looked deeper into the flames.

'Well, I wanted to get to know this country better. I was here on holiday with my wife and children many years ago and we liked it very much. We always have this dream to buy a little farm somewhere to keep goats and grow organic vegetables. Maybe I could even start a little business of my own. Would you come to work for me, ha?'

Niall smiled a tired smile and shook his head.

'I'm going to be a professional cyclist in France, like Stephen Roche.'

Wasserman smiled and nodded. He felt the clothes to see if they were dry.

'If that's the case, then I suggest we get on with your training!'

They stood up and dressed themselves again. Wasserman smothered the fire in damp ferns and stamped on it to make sure it was quite dead, then they picked up the bikes and kicked their way back through the camouflaged path to the muddy track.

'The forestry people should be starting work in an hour or two,' Wasserman said. 'We will just keep going at an easy pace till we meet someone, ja?'

They mounted and set off downhill, freewheeling with lazy care along the driest patches of the track that wound in big loops back into the uncropped forest patch below.

Niall was surprised how fresh he felt now, and Wasserman was very chirpy, whistling some complicated classical piece as he stood on the pedals to ride over the worst bumps.

'There's no chance they might come looking for us again?' Niall wondered.

Wasserman laughed, his head turning to follow a little band of squabbling forest birds that shot across the path only feet in front of their faces.

'If they have any sense at all, and even such dumbheads must have a little, they will all be hiding in a deep, dark cellar somewhere!'

After about half an hour of coasting downhill like this, they came to the level main road without having seen any forestry people on the way.

'Which way do we go?' Niall asked, looking left and right along the deserted dew-wet road.

Wasserman looked around at the sky.

'That is east,' he said, indicating the sun. 'And since we seem to be in the Wicklow mountains somewhere, we must head north towards the city. This way.'

He turned left and pedalled on, with Niall close behind. The road ran flat for a mile or so, then began to descend, allowing them to relax and pick up speed at the same time.

'We must surely meet somebody soon,' said Wasserman.

'I hope so!' Niall agreed. 'My stomach's roaring for a decent feed of rashers an' eggs an' bread an' butter!'

'Mine too! And I would very much like to have a shower. Come — let's get going!'

They spun their legs faster and began racing downwards, swooping round the bends and crouching low over the handlebars. They zoomed round a wide, cambered curve and found themselves scorching down a long, straight stretch that cut a clean line through the pines on either side.

Suddenly, at a crossroads about half a mile ahead, the three

126

police cars that held the captive gang emerged from the left and disappeared downhill at a furious speed.

Wasserman and Niall waved arms and shouted after them, but the cars dwindled and vanished in seconds.

'Verdammte Scheisse!' Wasserman spat after them.

'D'you think they're supposed to be looking for us?' Niall asked him.

'I can't think of any other reason for so many policemen to be so far from the comforts of the city!'

They raced on and down, swishing through the cool shadows between the walls of trees, then out into the bright sunlight burning across patches of empty mountain bog, and then back into the green shadows again.

A distant roaring sound began to grow louder around them and they slowed to listen and to look around for its source. It built up steadily till it felt as though it was all around them, but they could see nothing until Niall looked up and saw a helicopter fly low across the narrow band of sky above the tree-lined road. He raised his hand to wave but it was too late even as the thought left his mind for his arm.

'They *are* looking for us!' he shouted above the dying din.

Wasserman laughed.

'The problem is they don't seem to know that they must be looking for two cyclists. Let's just forget about them, eh? We are in the process of rescuing ourselves and doing a better job of it too!'

They pressed on and down, till the descent finally bottomed out somewhat and the road became flatter and straighter. The forests fell away, and now there were a few fields on either side with grazing animals in them. Wasserman squinted around thoughtfully.

'I seem to know this place,' he said.

Niall suddenly pointed ahead and stood up on the pedals.

'Look!'

Ahead of them, at the end of a short drive that led off the road onto a large gravel-surfaced car park, was a substantial house. Signs stuck out from high on its walls, and a huge one arched across the driveway entrance. Hotel Lomas, it said.

Wasserman took both hands from the handlebars and clapped them together in delight.

'I knew it! This is the place we come to every Sunday for lunch!'

He sprinted ahead and veered under the arched sign. Niall followed and they crunched across the gravel car park to the front steps of the house, where both abandoned the bikes heedlessly before bounding in through the double glass doors.

There was nobody at the reception desk and no sounds of anyone astir.

'Hello!' Wasserman called. 'Anyone awake yet?'

Nothing happened.

'Hello there!' he shouted, and rang the little bell at the desk.

Somewhere down the end of the entrance hall there was a bump and a dull clang. Then a plumpish, balding man with a thick black moustache and a shiny forehead emerged from what appeared to be the kitchen. He looked irritable at first, pulling down his rolled up shirt sleeves, but he suddenly became surprised and confused when he saw the pair standing in the entrance hall.

'Herr Wasserman ... this is unexpected! We're just getting breakfast ready ...'

He looked helplessly at Niall and Wasserman standing before him, scruffy and tousled and tired, but beaming with relief.

'Is something wrong?' he asked them.

'Something was very wrong!' Wasserman told him happily. 'But it's all right now, Anthony!'

The man was none the wiser for this information and stared blankly at them.

'Well then ... can I do something for you, gentlemen?' he inquired.

'Yes, you can,' Wasserman answered. Niall could tell by his tone that he was well used to having other people do things for him. 'We would like breakfast, please, Anthony. Double helpings of everything. And could I have a pot of strong coffee immediately, please. We'll wait in the dining room. Come, Niall.'

Wasserman led Niall into a richly furnished spacious room where six or seven tables were neatly set for breakfast. The bewildered Anthony disappeared back to the kitchen to do what he was bid.

'Nice man,' Wasserman explained to Niall as they sat down gratefully. 'He's the owner.'

After a short wait, Anthony began bringing them what they wanted — food. Fruit juice, grapefruit, bread, butter, marmalade, cereals, porridge, pots of tea and coffee, then bacon, eggs and sausages, then more of the same, and more again. To every offer of choice made by Anthony, Wasserman simply nodded as he ate, so they had everything brought to them without further question.

Once the more serious pangs of starvation had been soothed in his stomach, Niall had a thought.

'Shouldn't we ring the guards and let them know we're okay?'

Wasserman chewed and swallowed before answering.

'And let them spoil our feast of thanksgiving? They can wait another few minutes. Besides, I think they need as much practice as they can get in searching for people.'

Niall filled his mouth again in agreement.

When they had both finished stuffing themselves, they sat back to breathe more easily. Some residents began to drift in, eyeing them curiously.

'Would you like anything else?' inquired Anthony, who had now put on his jacket and was doing a very professional job of hiding his huge curiosity as to what these two were doing here at such an unearthly hour and in such a dishevelled condition.

'Yes,' said Wasserman meditatively. 'A Havana cigar, I think, just to round things off. Any Davidoffs left?'

The cigar was duly produced, cut and lit, and Wasserman sucked at it like a baby sucking its bottle.

'I think the time has come to make that phone call now,' he announced.

He went out to the reception desk and returned a few minutes later. Niall used the time to devour Wasserman's unwanted bread and marmalade.

'They'll be here in a matter of minutes,' Wasserman informed him. 'Perhaps we should greet them outside on the steps.'

Mr Anthony hovered at a respectful but carefully observant distance as they went out.

'We're expecting some friends,' Wasserman told him. 'Oh, about the bill — I'm afraid I left home in a bit of a hurry and didn't bring my credit cards. I'll settle up next time, if that's all right.'

Mr Anthony gave a single silent nod.

Niall and Wasserman sprawled on the sunlit steps, both on the verge of sleep after the night of exertions and the breakfast.

'I'll have to think of some way of thanking you properly for what you did,' Wasserman mused through a writhing stream of smoke.

Niall pulled his knees up to his chin and rested his head on them.

'All I want is to get my bike back again.'

A cavalcade of cars, some with garda markings, came tearing down the road from the direction of the hills and flew into the car park in front of them, sending pebbles flying in all directions as they skidded and scraped to a halt. Uniformed men and detectives leapt out and walked quickly up to them, just as Mr Anthony and some of the early breakfasting hotel guests came scampering out to see what all the commotion was about.

'Wasserman? Niall Quinn?' demanded one of the detectives.

Wasserman blew a smoke ring and nodded. The detective turned to shout at another officer still in one of the cars.

'It's them! Tell them to call it off!'

The man in the car lifted a microphone and spoke into it.

'Eh ... will all of your friends be requiring breakfast too?' Mr Anthony inquired apprehensively of Wasserman.

Paudge and Katy and her father, as red-eyed with tiredness as the pair on the steps, pushed their way through the policemen. Niall stood up but was nearly knocked over again as Katy threw herself on him.

'Safe and sound, eh Niall?' said her father.

Niall nodded exhaustedly as he extricated himself from Katy's assault, which he found acutely embarrassing in front of all the people watching. But as soon as he was free, Paudge did exactly the same thing to him.

'Did you ring your folks yet?' Katy's father reminded him once the scene was over. Wasserman was already giving the detectives his account of the kidnap and the flight.

'Not yet,' admitted Niall. 'I'd better do it now I suppose.'

He went into the hotel while Katy and Paudge threw all their previous reservations about each other to the winds and did a little dance together on the steps.

'Seems to have been the hero of the piece, that young lad,' one of the detectives said to Katy's father after hearing what Wasserman had to say.

'I don't think he's feeling very heroic at the moment.'

Niall re-emerged through the onlooking hotel guests, some of whom had brought their cornflakes or their coffee out with them.

'Everything all right, then?' inquired Katy.

Niall looked at them all with a wry half-smile.

'They thought I was upstairs in bed.'

14

Changes

NIALL AND PAUDGE both got a bit of a surprise the next time they saw each other.

It was ten days later, all of which Niall had spent in bed recovering from the effects of his adventures, then recovering from some kind of a fever he developed as an aftereffect, and then recovering from the effects of the massive doses of antibiotics his doctor had insisted he swallow, and which turned out to be ten times more debilitating than everything else.

When he finally got out of bed and wobbled downstairs, he was miraculously cured by a stunning vision in the hall. There, leaning against the wall, was a gleaming silver-framed racing bike of the kind used by all the top professionals, except in a smaller version. Over the top tube was draped a selection of dazzling attire as worn by the heroes of the sport — several brilliantly coloured racing jerseys, long shorts in wet-look material, skintights, racing socks and caps, and on the floor, a pair of sleek racing shoes.

Niall crashed in through the kitchen door, wild-eyed with excitement, and his mother nearly fell into the sinkful of dishes.

'Oh my God!' she gasped, holding a soapy hand over her thumping heart. She'd taken two weeks holidays since the kidnap drama to keep a guilty eye on Niall's convalescence.

'Where'd that bike and the gear come from?' Niall demanded.

She dried her hands on a dish towel before advancing determinedly on him.

'Niall, you are not well enough to be up and around, and especially not half naked!' she told him with emphasis on every word, and turned him back towards the stairs and bed.

'Where'd they come from?' he insisted, breaking free to fondle the items in question.

His mother pushed him up the stairs.

'Your Mr Wasserman brought them as a thank you for what you did, while you were half-dead with the fever. He'll be coming back in a day or two to talk to you again.'

Niall allowed himself to be incarcerated in the bed again, preferring to conserve his energy for later things rather than use it all up in an argument.

After lunch, when his mother went shopping and the house was empty, he got up, dressed himself in the racing gear, and went cruising like a god round the local streets on the stunning new bike.

Paudge was shocked to a standstill at the sight of him.

'I thought you were still half-dead! Where d'you get that machine an' all the gear?!'

'I was. Wasserman left it in for me. Magic, isn't it!'

Paudge found it so painfully magical, he was speechless as he inspected the whole ensemble with reverence.

'You been sick too?' Niall asked him. 'You look different. Thin.'

Paudge unbent himself proudly to allow Niall a better view of his transformed person. Ten days of severe self-discipline bordering on cruelty had wiped all but a pound or two of the slack chubbiness from his frame, and he had just that morning repeated Katy's earlier performance by spending his life savings on new jeans, a new sweat shirt, and a very sharp-looking jacket. He looked positively athletic, and felt great, if a bit hungry.

'Whad'jou do to yourself?' Niall wondered.

'I just felt it was time for a change,' Paudge shrugged with a smile. 'I lost a few pounds of weight, that's all. Any word of your other bike?'

Niall shook his head.

'All the bikes up at that farm place got burned to bits. Da had a look through what was left, but he says he couldn't see anything that could've been mine.'

'Maybe they'd sold it already,' suggested Paudge.

'I hope so. I'd rather somebody was using it than it just ended up a hunk of burnt metal.'

'When you going to court?'

'Court? The cops never said anything about court when they called in.'

'For the trial. You're going to be the star witness. Didn't you know?'

Niall shook his head, puzzled. Paudge pulled a piece of a newspaper page from his inside pocket and gave it to him.

'It was all over the papers. They called you a hero. They've even got your picture in. Your folks must've given them one.'

Niall grinned with amazement as he read what was said about him and what had happened up there in the mountains.

'Chee!' he muttered quietly.

'They got all the kidnappers, and all the bike thieves except one. They're still looking for him,' Paudge explained.

'Which one?'

'The ringleader. His name is P.J. Donoghue.'

Niall handed back the newspaper page.

'Well, I'm glad they didn't get him, an' I hope they don't. He seemed like a decent skin, even if he was the boss an' he sold my bike. Maybe he couldn't get a job and had to steal bikes to feed his family.'

Paudge gave him a sceptical look as he put the cutting away again.

'Maybe he was just a crook who didn't care what he did to other people as long he got money anyhow.'

Niall wasn't listening. He was staring over Paudge's left shoulder with narrowed eyes. Paudge turned to see what was attracting his attention so powerfully. Coming towards them, on the other side of the road, was a girl they didn't recognise but who was nevertheless strangely familiar. She was dressed in an up-to-the-minute and obviously split new outfit of black with brilliant lemons and pinks, and her red hair, swept up and back in an elegantly dramatic style, added a perfect dash of understated outrageousness to her appearance.

'It's Katy!' Paudge breathed as she closed in on them. 'Where's her glasses?'

Katy it was. And without her glasses, even though she was perfectly able to steer a straight course and avoid obstacles, she was having a slight problem reading the reaction on Niall's face at that distance. Not that she had any doubts at all as to the perfection of her presentation, for like everything she had ever set her mind to, she'd got it right first time. Attention to detail is the essence of quality in all things, her father had made that almost the first entry in her earliest memory. What was concerning her now was that maybe the new Katy — Katherine — wasn't Niall's style at all.

The two lads continued to gaze in speechless wonder as she drew level with them, and made no attempt to hail her or otherwise arrest her progress as she began to pass on. Katherine clamped Katy's jaw tightly shut in case she gave in to the temptation to turn on them and yell: EEJITS! You're supposed to whistle or shout hello or run after me, not just stand there like DUMMIES!

Instead, she surrendered to the inevitable and did the job herself.

'Hi, Paudge. Hi, Niall.' She stopped at the edge of the pavement and spoke to them across the width of the road. 'That's a lovely new bike. You must be a lot better if the doctor's let you go out cycling.'

Niall stared across the street into her eyes. He hadn't seen them without glasses in front of them for years, and now he found himself locked onto the gaze of a total stranger.

A car passed between them, jolting both Niall and Paudge out of their trance-like condition.

'Yeah ... yeah,' Niall agreed with her. 'I am.'

Katherine realised this was it. If the conversation fizzled out and she walked on, he would probably feel too intimidated by her new persona to come after her, then and probably forever after. She'd read about a similar tragedy in the advice page of one of Cousin Fiona's magazines.

She stepped across the road.

'Actually,' she began, once she was directly in front of them, 'I was just on my way over to your place anyway. To see how you were. And to ask if you'd like to come to the cinema once you're better. There's a really good film on this week.'

Paudge watched them as their black-pupiled gazes locked again. He was surprised to find his own heartbeat was drumming away at an unusually high rate. Probably the shock of seeing Katy like this. So different. Even her shape had altered dramatically. Curves and things had suddenly appeared out of nowhere. She looked more like a model than a girl.

Niall swallowed once or twice, and when he answered his voice sounded funny and dry from breathing through his open mouth.

'Sure. Great. When d'you want to go?'

She shrugged.

'Well, if you're well enough ... how about this evening?'

'Right. I'll go home and change.'

He started to swing his leg over the bicycle.

'I'll come with you and wait, will I?' she said, more as a statement of intention than a question. Her eyes made it clear she wasn't going to let him out of her sight at this crucial stage.

Niall looked at her, then turned and thrust the bike into Paudge's unexpecting grasp.

'You can play with it for a while, Paudge.' He turned back to Katherine. 'We'll walk.'

They were almost at the other side of the street, when Niall turned round to warn the speechless Paudge:

'But mind you don't let anybody rob this one!'

Paudge waited till they had disappeared round the corner before turning his bewildered attention to the gleaming machine in his hands. It's really happened this time, he told himself. Niall's flipped.

Eventually, he swung himself onto the bike and cruised away, cautiously at first, but then picking up speed as the exhilaration crackled up through his limbs from the pedals and the handlebars, till he was so consumed by the feeling he totally forgot his astonishment at what had just taken place.

A few streets further on, the twins came whirring towards him. They freewheeled as they caught sight of him, just as amazed at his transformation as he had been at Katy's. He caught the surprise on their faces and gave them a nonchalant B-movie wave as they sailed past, lips open. When he looked over his shoulder, they had turned and were racing after him.

He let them catch up.

'Where d'jou get that bike, Paudge?'

'Where d'jou get the new clothes? They make you look awful slim!'

'Hey! Have you seen Niall out yet?'

'Yeah,' he told them, not taking his eyes from the road ahead. 'He's gone off to the pictures with Katy.'

The twins stopped pedalling and let him surge ahead. Katy?! their eyes said in dismay and disbelief as they stared at each other.

But then they both turned to watch Paudge pedalling easily from them, splendid in his new finery and on his glinting silent steed.

With an exchange of impish looks and flicks of the head, the girls rose on their pedals and set off in pursuit.

'Wait, Paudge!' they chorused. 'Wait for us! We're coming with you!'

Other books from
THE O'BRIEN PRESS

HORSE THIEF
Hugh Galt

Rory's beloved old mare disappears. Then three girls discover a racehorse kidnapped and held for ransom near their home. These two stories interweave into a nail-biting story, full of action and thrills.

Paperback £3.99

THE CHIEFTAIN'S DAUGHTER
Sam McBratney

A boy fostered with a remote Irish tribe 1500 years ago becomes involved in a local feud and with the fate of his beloved Frann, the Chieftain's daughter.

Paperback £3.99

MISSING SISTERS
Gregory Maguire

In a fire in a holiday home, Alice's favourite nun is injured and disappears to hospital. Back at the orphanage, Alice is faced with difficult choices, then a surprise enters her life when she meets a girl called Miami.

Paperback £3.99

CHEROKEE
Creina Mansfield

Gene's grandfather Cherokee is a famous jazz musician and Gene travels the world with him. He loves the life and his only ambition is to be a musician too. But his aunt has other plans!

Paperback £3.99

COULD THIS BE LOVE? I WONDERED
Marilyn Taylor

First love for Jackie is full of anxiety, hope, discovery. Kev *seems* to be interested in her, but is he really? Why is he withdrawn? And what can she do about Sinead?

Paperback £3.99

UNDER THE HAWTHORN TREE
Marita Conlon-McKenna

Eily, Michael and Peggy are left without parents when the Great Famine strikes. They set out on a long and dangerous journey to find the great-aunts their mother told them about in her stories.

Paperback £3.99

WILDFLOWER GIRL
Marita Conlon-McKenna

Peggy, from *Under the Hawthorn Tree*, is now thirteen and must leave Ireland for America. After a terrible journey on board ship, she arrives in Boston. What kind of life will she find there?

Hardback £6.95 Paperback £4.50

THE BLUE HORSE
Marita Conlon-McKenna

When their caravan burns down, Katie's family must move to live in a house on a new estate. But for Katie, this means trouble. Is she strong enough to deal with the new situation?

Paperback £3.99

NO GOODBYE
Marita Conlon-McKenna

When their mother leaves, the four children and their father must learn to cope without her. It is a trial separation between their parents. Gradually, they all come to deal with it in their own way.

Paperback £3.99

THE HUNTER'S MOON
Orla Melling

Cousins Findabhair and Gwen defy an ancient law at Tara, and Findabhair is abducted. In a sequence of amazing happenings, Gwen tries to retrieve her cousin from the Otherworld.

Paperback £3.99

THE SINGING STONE
Orla Melling

A gift of ancient books sparks off a visit to Ireland by a young girl. Her destiny becomes clear – *she* has been chosen to recover the four treasures of the Tuatha de Danann. All her ingenuity and courage are needed.

Paperback £3.99

THE DRUID'S TUNE
Orla Melling

In the adventure of their lives, two teenage visitors to Ireland are hurled into the ancient past and become involved in the wild and heroic life of Cuchulainn and in the fierce battle of the Táin.

Paperback £4.50

STRONGBOW
Morgan Llywelyn

The dramatic story of the Norman conquest of Ireland in the twelfth century, as told by Strongbow and by Aoife Mac Murrough, the Irish princess whom he married.

Paperback £3.99

BRIAN BORU
Morgan Llywelyn

The exciting, real-life story of High King Brian Boru and of tenth-century Ireland brought vividly to life.

Paperback £3.95

THE CASTLE IN THE ATTIC
Elizabeth Winthrop

There is a strange legend attached to the model castle given to William by Mrs Phillips. William is drawn into the story when the silver knight comes to life.

Paperback £3.99

THE BATTLE FOR THE CASTLE
Elizabeth Winthrop

The sequel to *The Castle in the Attic*. William must use his wits to face an evil force intent on the total destruction of the world. As he battles to save the castle, William discovers that there is more than one way to become a hero.

Paperback £3.99

THE SECRET CITY
Carolyn Swift

When Nuala and Kevin visit the hidden city of Petra in the mysterious land of the Bedouin, they find themselves involved in intrigue and strange happenings.

Paperback £3.99

ON SILENT WINGS
Don Conroy

After his mother's death, a young barn owl is left alone to survive in a world he does not yet know. Who is the Emperor of Fericul who threatens him?

Paperback £4.99

CARTOON FUN
Don Conroy

An action-packed how-to-draw book which shows you how to draw your own cartoons – with spectacular results! People, faces, monsters . . . and more.

Paperback £4.95

WILDLIFE FUN

How to draw animals – realistically and in cartoon – and lots of interesting things about them. Full of fun and fascination.

Paperback £4.99

THE TÁIN
Liam MacUistin

The great classic Celtic tale, full of the excitement of the battle, and ending with the terrible fight to the death between best friends Cuchulainn and Ferdia.

Hardback £5.95 Paperback £3.99

CELTIC MAGIC TALES
Liam Mac Uistin

Four magical legends from Ireland's Celtic past vividly told – heroic quests, great deeds, fantasy and fun.

Paperback £3.99

HEROIC TALES FROM THE ULSTER CYCLE
Curriculum Development Unit

Classic stories from the ancient Irish legends – Cuchulainn and Queen Maeve's Tain.

Paperback £3.99

AMELIA

Siobhán Parkinson

Almost thirteen, Amelia Pim, daughter of a wealthy Dublin Quaker family, loves frocks and parties – but now she must learn to live with poverty and the disgrace of a mother arrested for suffragette activities.

Paperback £3.99

ORDER FORM

These books are available from your local bookseller. In case of difficulty order direct from THE O'BRIEN PRESS

Please send me the books as marked

I enclose cheque / postal order for £........... (+ 50p P&P per title)

OR please charge my credit card ☐ Access / Mastercard ☐ Visa

Card number ☐☐☐☐ ☐☐☐☐ ☐☐☐☐ ☐☐☐☐

EXPIRY DATE ☐ ☐ ☐ ☐

Name: ....Tel: ....

Address: ....

....

Please send orders to: THE O'BRIEN PRESS, 20 Victoria Road, Dublin 6.
Tel: (Dublin) 4923333 Fax: (Dublin) 4922777